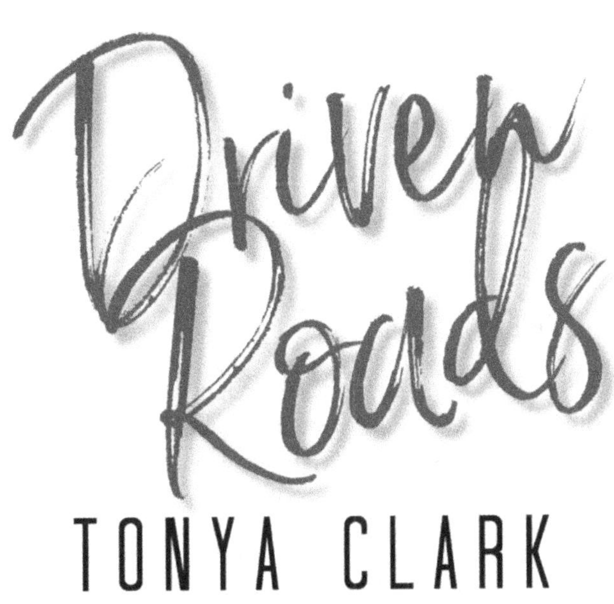

TONYA CLARK

Print Edition ISBN 978-1-949243-70-3

Page Overall Images: Tonya Clark Photography- All About the Covers

Models: Sean Brady & Mikky Clark

Cover Designer: Tonya Clark

Editor: Ink It Out Editing

I have two amazing daughters who every day inspire me. My youngest, the inspiration behind this story, surprises me daily on the hurtles she has to over come being deaf. My oldest, her kindness towards everyone she meets and taking on any adventure without fear. They are both the reasons I continue to do all that I do. I love you both very much and couldn't do any of this without your support.

CHAPTER ONE

JORDYN

Precision is timing, and in my world timing is everything. A person's sight is by far the most important sense we can have. I've learned that losing any of our senses can be life-altering, but every day since the accident I'm thankful it wasn't my sight. Losing my sense of sound, though, life changing.

My world revolves around music. My mom says I've been humming since before I could talk. Music is a part of me, and nothing will take it from me, I've just had to work a little harder to feel it.

The last sound I heard was the sound of metal twisting and tearing all around me, glass shattering and my mom's scream, then silence.

Some say silence is peaceful, fifteen years ago I would have thought you had lost your mind. My life revolved around sound. The soft sound of a piano, the strumming of a guitar, the solid beat of the drums. Music was my world.

One night and one person's very wrong decision, that's

all it took to lose it all. Now all I have are my memories, and as I get older I try to find that sound in my memories to overshadow the last sounds I heard, but the reminder is always there.

I have to feel the beat within now. The beat of the drums with the pulse of my heart, the strum of the guitar against my skin, both sending vibrations through my body.

People ask me all of the time if I'm angry that I lost my hearing. My answer is pretty simple. Yes, at first I was, but now I'm grateful that I was able to learn how to feel the world around me, not just see it.

My love for music is still huge, probably even more now than when I could hear. Now I get to feel it and that makes me so much better than I was when I could hear and it has brought me to where I am now. Yes, it may have taken a little longer, but my dream of recording is happening, all thanks to Mr. Emly, the only voice coach my mom could find that was up for the challenge to take on a deaf singer.

If that accident wouldn't have happened, I would never have met Mr. Emly. I don't think I'd be ready for all of this if it would have happened any earlier in my life.

Standing in the studio, looking through the clear glass of the window separating myself from the control room, I feel my nerves starting to jump around. Mr. Emly is talking to the producer and I'm patiently waiting here alone, with a microphone. I don't have my guitar so my hands feel antsy. All I can do is stand here and wait. Silence hasn't felt this lonely in a long time.

The gentleman sitting behind the control board signals for me to grab the headphones sitting on the stool next to me. I shyly smile and slightly shake my head. I have no need for them.

My eyes are starting to burn, I think I've refused to blink in fear that I'm going to miss Mr. Emly's sign that the song is starting. He has taught me how to feel the beat, but when the music is in a different room and you are in a sound room where there can't be any background music, things become a little difficult. We have been preparing for this and the sign he'll give me, I'm just afraid if I blink I may miss it.

The gentleman sitting behind the board turns around and says something to the producer, but without seeing his mouth I've no idea what he may be saying, I'm sure he is voicing his disapproval of my defiance over wearing the headphones. Mr. Emly signs as he answers, explaining to the man that I'm deaf and don't need the headphones. I appreciate him signing to bring me into the conversation. Another thing I adore about this man, he learned sign language just so he could communicate with me. I laugh as the man whips around in his chair again with eyes wide in disbelief, and it helps settle my nerves a little.

I firmly believe in the saying "everything happens for a reason." My family would never have met Mr. Emly if it wasn't for me losing my hearing. If I wouldn't have had him as my coach, I don't think I would have become the singer that I am. I wouldn't appreciate the sounds I can't hear the way I do now.

I'm not sure how long I've been standing here, but I swear my legs are going numb. Of course, that may be because I'm nervous and they haven't stopped shaking since I walked in. I contemplate using the stool and sitting while I wait, however,

I don't want to look like I'm bored or being impatient to the producer on the other side of the glass. He's a friend of Mr. Emly's, and I want to make sure I'm sending all the right signs of how appreciative I am that he is giving me this chance.

The door opens up behind the two men. I can't see who is entering, but both men turn at the same time to the new addition into the studio. Curiosity is definitely piqued right now. Were we waiting on someone else this whole time? Who else would need to be here?

Mr. Emly shakes the man's hand and his body shifts just enough for me to get a look at the new addition to the studio. My knees about buckle. It's Asher James, lead singer of the number one country band, Driven Roads.

Everyone is turned and looking at me now. Fingers are being pointed, smiles and nods are all I'm getting. Talk about feeling like a fish in a bowl. I can't make out what any of them are saying because I can't seem to stop staring at the most breathtaking guy I've ever seen. I should be trying to read their lips, but I can't manage to shift my eyes. He is nodding at something they are saying, but his eyes are locked with mine, and that sexy, melt-your-heart half-smile he has is making my chest hum.

What's the most popular singer, in the most widely known country band, doing here in the studio that I'm about to record in? I'm in such a trance I haven't even noticed Mr. Emly leave the group and walk into the room with me, that is until I jump and knock over the stool and headphones on it when he touches my arm.

I'm making a complete fool of myself in front of this guy. I step back and watch as Mr. Emly rights the stool and replaces the headphones. When he faces me again I see the small smile on his face that he's trying very hard to cover up.

"What's Asher James doing here?" I finally find my voice to ask.

"I didn't want to say anything to you but," his hands are moving in front of me, "you aren't only here to record for yourself, I found out the band Driven Roads is looking to add a female vocal to the group. Scott is their producer slash manager. He mentioned to me he was looking and I instantly thought of you. I didn't say anything because I didn't want to freak you out."

"Why would you think I would freak?" I sign back, looking down at the stool I knocked over earlier and rolling my eyes.

Mr. Emly smiles, "You're ready for this, Jordyn. I think you're exactly what they need."

I wish I had his confidence in myself right now. "So he's going to be listening as well?"

"Kind of the point," he signs.

Fantastic, I can't imagine what he's already thinking of me. I stood here gawking at him like every other starstruck female does I'm sure, and to top everything off, I knocked over the equipment in the room. I'm sure he isn't really impressed at the moment.

"Jordyn, get out of your head," he signs.

I chance another look into the other room and notice Asher and his producer in a conversation. I can't read anything they are saying, but one word did pop, *deaf*.

"Did you not tell him I'm deaf?" This time I speak the

question, for some reason feeling like I have to hide the signing now.

Mr. Emly, on the other hand, isn't hiding anything. "Jordyn," he signs, "you have an amazing voice, and if I didn't think you would be amazing I never would have suggested you. I know you are ready, you know you are ready, it's time you show them you are who they need."

Asher turns his attention back to us and catches me staring. I can't look away, though. His eyes are an electric blue and with brown hair to brighten them even more, they can easily put a person in a trance. Shaking my head slightly, I need to get a grip. There's no way I'm coming across as a professional, and I'm probably embarrassing Mr. Emly.

"I'm sorry. You are right, I'm ready," I sign.

A quick hug before he leaves the room, and once again I'm standing alone. I follow him with my eyes as he stands next to the producer once again. I refuse to look at Asher again. I need to focus. Mr. Emly gives some direction to the guy sitting behind the sound board and signals for me to get ready.

Closing my eyes, I take a couple deep breaths to settle my nerves. When I open them I concentrate only on my teacher and try to forget everyone else in the room. His finger begins to tap lightly against his thigh. One, my hand comes up to rest on my chest, just above my heart. Two, I take a breath. Three, we tap together, the music has started. My hand taps against my chest as his does against his thigh for me to find the beat of the song. I begin to count it off in my head and find the exact moment I'm to start in with the vocals.

Movement at Mr. Emly's side draws my attention away from him as Asher takes a couple steps closer to the sound board, as by getting closer to the glass he'd be able to hear something more. I'm not sure how to take the reaction, but I can't allow it to distract me. Mr. Emly is right, we've been working hard to get me here and I'm ready.

"Roads Taken" is the band's number one song right now. I understand now why that's the song Mr. Emly wanted me to sing. Asher's lips begin to move and I realize he is singing the song along with me on the other side of the glass. I've practiced this song for the past month, I know it inside and out, but watching Asher's lips move to the words almost trips me up, but I catch myself quickly and find myself singing along with him now.

You know those scenes in the movie, where two people meet and the room around them disappears leaving only them? Cheesy, I know, but that's completely what's happening right now. I don't recall singing half of the song, I've no idea how long I've been standing here, making a complete fool of myself just staring at Asher. I'm not watching for the reaction of the producer, or trying to read lips to see what is being said. I'm waiting to see a reaction from Asher, and I'm getting nothing. Just blue eyes trying to read the situation as I am.

A hand clasps down onto Asher's shoulder and his eyes break away from mine as he turns and talks to his producer. I blink a couple of times and look around the room on the other side of the glass. Mr. Emly is waving for me to come and join them. He's smiling but it's not giving away too much of what may be happening.

CHAPTER TWO

ASHER

I'm not sure if I agree with Scott on needing to bring in a female vocal to the group, but he seems to think that it will take us over the top. So instead of arguing with him, I've decided to humor him and show up today at the recording studio for a few minutes. Driven Roads has been having an amazing year. "Roads Taken" hit the charts and climbed to number one almost overnight. We do have Scott to thank for that. He has taken our band from playing in bars and small fairs, to sold-out stadiums in less than a year.

We've all made some very rapid changes in our lives, and have had to adjust quickly to the fame. Scott isn't slowing down, though. He thinks if we bring the female voice to the band, we'll have no problem staying on top.

Walking into the studio, Scott instantly turns. "Asher, I'm glad you showed up. Let me introduce you to a great friend of mine, Sean Emly."

Shaking the man's hand, I try to get a look at the

woman who is standing alone in the sound booth. I see a shade of a darker red colored hair, but the guys are blocking my view. Sean moves to the side slightly and I'm caught instantly by a pair of eyes that I can only describe as a white-blue color staring back at me in disbelief.

"Asher, that is Jordyn Collins," Scott points through the glass as both men turn and now look at the woman standing alone in the studio.

"I have to confess, she had no idea you were going to be here. I haven't mentioned anything to her. Excuse me for a minute," Sean steps away and walks into the room.

I watch as he touches the woman's arm and she jumps, knocking over the stool and everything on it. Her cheeks instantly turn red, and I find that I can't take my eyes off of her.

Nothing could have surprised me more than what happens next, though. Sean picks up the stool and I see the girl say something to him, but the surprise is when Sean's hands come up and begin moving in front of the woman. He is signing to her.

I look over at Scott with a questioning look. "There is one thing I haven't mentioned."

"And what would that be, Scott?" I ask a little sarcastically. It's pretty obvious what it is.

"Jordyn is deaf."

I know I must be looking at him as though he has sprouted a second head, because I'm pretty sure deaf still means what it always has. "What do you mean she is deaf?"

"Deaf means she can't hear, Asher." His smart ass remark has me rolling my eyes at him.

"I know what it means, Scott."

"Look, Sean is one of my oldest friends. That man's ear for music is beyond anyone I know. He missed his calling in this industry, but he wanted to teach, not produce. He has been talking about Jordyn for years. Let's just see what she can do."

This beautiful woman standing on the other side of the glass is deaf. The word keeps repeating itself in my head. I've watched her mouth move a couple of times so I know she can talk, but now the two of them are signing again and I feel a little jealous about not being a part of the conversation.

She nods, and turns her attention back to us in the room. Sean comes back out and gives me a small smile. I just nod back. I'm intrigued. She looks anywhere but at me, and her cheeks still have a tint of red to them.

"Okay, she's ready," Sean announces, and stands in front of the sound board. I can't imagine how she's feeling right now, with all four of us just staring at her, like she's going to do a trick behind the glass or something.

I'm mesmerized by her as I watch her hand come up to her chest and rest lightly above her heart. She closes her eyes for a brief second and takes a deep breath, I find myself taking one with her. She opens her eyes, her hand taps once lightly, and the music begins. I watch as her hand taps in beat with our number one song.

The voice that reaches my ears throughout the room through the sound system is smooth and controlled. There's no nervous shake in the voice, her tone is perfect and I can instantly see her standing on the stage. She was born to sing in front of millions.

I have to fight the need to go and enter the room with her, grab her hand and place it on my heart. Have her tap along with my beat. I take a step closer and find the sound board in my way. Before I know it, I'm singing the lyrics along with her.

Her eyes meet mine and I'm lost. I see her lips kick up in the slightest smile when she realizes I'm singing along with her. The song sounds like it was meant to be sung by the both of us. Her voice added to the words and music sends this song to an entirely new level.

"Now do you see what I've been saying, Asher?" Scott's voice breaks the spell between myself and Jordyn.

I can't look away, though. "You were right, Scott!"

His hand comes down onto my shoulder, "I see some amazing things happening in the future."

I'm finally able to pull my glaze away from Jordyn and look over at Scott. "What's next?"

Sean signals for Jordyn to come join us. I have to control a need to meet her at the door adjoining the two rooms.

She walks in with an unsure look on her face. She looks between Sean and Scott, but her eyes never land on me as she waits on someone to say something. Scott moves toward her, and I have to fight the need to step in front of him before he can reach her.

"Jordyn, I'm very impressed," Scott extends his hand to her with his business card.

Jordyn looks between his outstretched hand and Sean, almost like she's asking for reassurance.

Sean nods his head, with the proud teacher smile on his face.

I notice the slight shake in her hand as she reaches out and takes the card from Scott, "Thank you."

"Young lady, are you ready for your life to change? Because it's going to happen very quickly." Scott isn't hiding his excitement very well.

She looks over at Sean, and I watch as he signs to her, I'm going to guess interrupting what Scott had just said.

They continue signing back and forth, Scott and I just watch from the side. I wish I knew what they were saying, she has a concerned look in her eyes, instead of the excitement I'd expect to see at this moment.

"Look..." Scott interrupts them, "I know there are a lot of questions. Why don't the four of us meet for dinner tonight and talk then?"

Sean signs as Scott is talking, Jordyn's eyes are wide and unsure.

"I'd like that, thank you," her voice is smooth and soft.

Scott once again shakes her hand, then moves to shake the hand of his old friend. I use this moment to step up to Jordyn.

I extend out my hand to her and smile, how the hell are we going to communicate if Scott isn't around? I don't know sign language.

"It's nice to meet you, Asher."

I look over my shoulder with a questioning look to Sean.

"Just make sure you are looking at her when you talk, she is amazing at reading lips," Scott answers my questioning look.

I bring my eyes back to hers, "It's nice to meet you, too."

"Thank you for this opportunity."

Her hand is still in mine, and I'm fighting the need to pull her closer. "I think this is going to work perfectly."

Her smile widens, and it's at this moment I realize this isn't going to be easy. The need to have her in my arms is intense. My muscles want to defy everything my brain is saying, and pull her in tight against me. Probably not the best way to start things between us.

For the past year, women have done unthinkable things to get our attention. None of them we give a second glance to. Sure you smile, wave, stop a couple of times and sign an autograph or take a picture. They go insane, but honestly, I'm not sure any of us really see them, there are just too many. Time moves in slow motion and in hyper speed all at the same time. The crowds always look endless and yet, you are pulled through by security so quickly that if you blink it's over and you are tucked safely back in the bus or a building.

She looks down at our hands, and I feel the slight tug she gives as she tries to take her hand back. I let go instantly, but it is one of the hardest actions I've ever had to do.

"So, we'll meet you two later tonight," Sean's voice breaks in between us. His hands moving brings Jordyn's eyes away from mine.

She nods, following her teacher out of the room. "Thank you again," she comments before they disappear through the door.

"Play back the song, please," Scott gives the direction to the guy sitting behind the table.

Music fills the room and her voice, and surprisingly mine, flow in with it.

"She is going to be perfect for the group." Scott sounds extremely proud of himself and is giving me that *I told you so* look right now.

"I'm not going to say I agreed with you on this initially, but you were right, Scott, she's going to be perfect."

CHAPTER THREE

Following Mr. Emly out of the building, I'm still having a very hard time believing all of what just happened. I recorded for a producer, who just happens to work with the number one band in country music right now. Asher James, the band's lead singer, watched, and sang along with me. To top everything off, I think I'm being asked to join the group.

Once outside, I need to stop and take a couple deep breaths of fresh air. This isn't at all what I was expecting to happen today, and my brain isn't wrapping around all of the information very quickly. Looking back through the glass doors and into the building, I wonder if this is all a dream.

A bench to the side of the walkway looks inviting and a good place to sit before my very wobbly legs give out from under me and I make a fool of myself in front of everyone.

Quickly sitting, I rock slightly, my hands tucked between my knees, and wonder how did my life just change that fast? Mr. Emly sits down beside me. He doesn't say anything, we just sit.

I just sang a song with Asher James, one of the most sought out men in country music. They just offered me a spot in the band. How is all of this happening? It just keeps repeating through my head.

"Jordyn, stop." Mr. Emly's hands come out in front of me, drawing my attention to him.

"Stop what?" I ask.

"You are trying to figure out how this is all happening to you. I can see it written all over your face. You have a gift and it's time the world was blessed with hearing it. That's why I set this up. I knew you were ready. This has been your dream for as long as I've known you. It's your time."

Mr. Emly has never tried to discourage me from becoming a singer. Even those days when things weren't being grasped that easily and I was ready to throw up my hands, he kept encouraging me to continue. I'd love to say that I dove head first into continuing my dreams after the accident, determined to be the singer I always dreamed of being. Like anyone who has had their life altered as I have, we have down moments. Moments where you don't believe in yourself and feel sorry for oneself. I'm no different, I've had a few of those moments, but Mr. Emly never quit on me and refused to let me quit on myself, regardless if it was in music, learning my new language, or mastering the art of lip reading, he has done nothing but encourage me to be my best.

This is another of those times. He is right. All I've ever wanted to do was sing in front of fans, on a big stage. He has given me that gift.

"I'm sorry, I'm so grateful for what you have done for me. I think I'm just still in shock. It was almost a little too easy. Famous singer walks in, I sing, bam, now a member of one of the top country bands in the world. Not as easy to catch the mind up with the actions. There is no way I'll ever be able to say thank you enough for what you have done for me just now."

A slight sheen of tear in his eyes has me choked up as well. "No thank you is necessary, Jordyn. This is what we have been working toward. Fifteen years ago, you walked into my music room and even at the age of ten, you were very determined to work around the fact that you could no longer hear the music but still wanted to sing. The sadness I saw that day in your eyes was almost unbearable. You were describing to me what you missed the most about hearing the sounds of all the instruments. I knew then you were special. I just needed to teach you how to feel the sounds. You are going to be amazing."

There was no stopping the tears from rolling down my cheeks. "But..." he continued, "you cannot stop being the amazing woman you have become. For a slight moment I saw your hesitation with them knowing you were deaf. You stopped signing. Jordyn, there is no reason to hide from anyone the fact that you can't hear. It's going to be hard, your life is about to do a massive turn around. The fame and the popularity is going to be very hard to balance at first."

He is referring to the moment in the studio when I saw

the disbelief on Asher's face when he found out I was deaf. I stopped signing. I didn't want him to judge so quickly just because I couldn't hear. That was a bad mistake on my part.

"I understand what you are saying, it was a bad moment. The whole situation took me a little by surprise. You're right, it was wrong of me."

"Jordyn, that's not what I'm saying. I get it, but you used to tell me not to treat you like someone who couldn't hear, to treat you like any other singer I'd teach. You need to do the same for yourself. Just be yourself."

I'm not embarrassed that I can't hear, it's just that I don't want people to judge me before they know. It's happened a lot, but he is right.

"Look, head home, take a little time to think everything through before we meet up with them again tonight," he stands up and stretches a hand out to me to help me up.

Taking it, I stand and hug the man that has always believed in me. He has been like another father figure to me and there are no words to express how lucky I feel that my mom was able to find him.

"Come on, I'll walk you to your car," he pulls away and starts in the direction of the parking lot.

Walking into my little apartment I stop just inside the door and look around. I want to text my mom, dad, and my brother, mostly I want to tell Megan, but I don't really want to say anything until I'm sure. Pulling Scott's business card out of my back pocket, I sit down on the couch and stare at it. The word producer/manager pops. Closing my eyes, I'm instantly reminded of the bright blue eyes of Asher James. The way they held mine while we sang together, through the glass. I read amazement, shock, intrigue and it may just be a wishful thinking but a need as well in them. What woman doesn't want to believe that Asher wants them? I'm a little embarrassed to say I'm just like every other woman out there who has seen that man.

I've always wanted to be on the large stage, performing in front of thousands of fans, but this is something a little different. I'll be joining into a group that is already huge. No working up to the thousands, but stepping onto a stage in front of thousands, in very large stadiums and part of a world I can't even imagine. Am I ready for all of this?

Mr. Emly is right. I've wanted this ever since I was a little girl. I'd set up a little stage in my room and call my parents and my brother, Justin, in and perform for them. Being my best friend, Megan always had to sit through my little show. Four people, five if you include Mr. Emly, that is all I have performed for, which is a lot smaller number than the amount of people that are fans of Driven Roads.

My phone vibrates in my pocket. Pulling it out, I see Megan's picture on the screen. I'm not sure if I should even read it. I want to tell someone, but I'm not sure if I'm jumping the gun on letting the news out.

Megan: How did it go?

Megan: Are you still there?

Megan: Are you going to be a huge star?

I laugh to myself as the questions fly through text after text. She is hard to ignore.

Me: We are meeting again tonight for dinner to discuss some details. I'll text you when I'm home.

It's killing me not to mention that I just sang with Asher James, she would freak out, and if I know my friend at all, she would be here and begging to join us for dinner tonight.

Megan: That's all the detail you are going to give me?

She is my best friend, and I tell her everything, but I think for now this is something I need to keep to myself until I find out more tonight. I don't want to find out that I read everything very wrong today in the studio, tell everyone, get them excited and then tell them I was wrong.

Me: Not much detail to give right now. I promise I'll text as soon as I get home after dinner tonight.

I wait as the little dots wave on the screen that she is responding.

Megan: I know you slayed it, text me the second you walk in the door.

Me: Promise.

Megan, and I have known each other since the first grade. After the accident she spent days at my house, her mom even let her miss a week of school right after I got home from the hospital to help me out. Together, we learned sign language and without her I don't think I would have made it through public school. I didn't want to go to a special school for the deaf, so she volunteered to be my translator in all of my classes. Keeping today's events from her and what happened with Asher is killing me. She may kill me when she finds out what happened and that I didn't say anything to her.

. . .

Mr. Emly is waiting for me when I walk up to the restaurant. "Are you ready?" he signs.

My nerves haven't stopped jumping since I walked out of the studio today and now they are threatening to turn me around and send me home. "I'm as ready as I'm going to be."

Holding the door open for me to enter, I take a deep breath and walk in the restaurant. I feel him right behind me. I watch the hostess's mouth move and I'm assuming Mr. Emly answered the question because we are now being led through the dining area.

We stop at a large table where Scott and Asher are already sitting. Another gentleman, wearing a suit, is there that wasn't at the studio today along with five more guys dressed more casually, I recognize them as the members of the group. I didn't think the whole band would be here tonight. I take a step back only to bump into Mr. Emly behind me. He nudges me forward and pulls out one of the chairs for me, a sign for me to take a seat.

Looking over my shoulder, I give him a smile and take the seat. I settle myself and watch as he takes the seat next to me. I'm not ready to make eye contact with the rest of the men around the table, especially one of them. I feel everyone's eyes on me and so that I don't come across as rude, I slowly make my way around the table and smile at each of them.

I'm trying very hard not to have a fan girl moment. I'm sitting at a table with the entire Driven Roads band. I have to be professional, I keep telling myself, when all I want to do is text Megan. This is unreal.

My eyes finally fall onto Asher, and I think I've stopped breathing. He has changed into a black button-up shirt, his hair is hanging slightly down his forehead because of the unruly wave to it. Dark hair, against very bright blue eyes. A dangerous combination on any man. His black cowboy hat is hanging from the back of his chair and I can only imagine the sight he presents when he has it on.

A tap on my arm breaks my eye contact with him. Before I turn my attention back to Mr. Emly, I catch his band mate saying something to him and they both laugh. Maybe I stared a little too much at him and they both noticed. I feel my cheeks heat up from embarrassment.

"Jordyn, Scott wants to introduce you to Steven Moningham, the owner of the record label," he signs, and I watch as his mouth moves as well.

I bring my attention to Scott and then over to the man I first noticed when I walked up to the table who was in the suit. "It's nice to meet you, Mr. Moningham," I sign as I speak.

"Please, call me Steven. It's nice to meet you as well, Jordyn. Scott hasn't stopped talking about you since he called me this afternoon," he points over at Asher, "and neither has he."

My eyes go wide with shock as I look over at Asher once again. He shrugs, "I was impressed."

"Thank you," is all I can say. I'm finding myself speechless.

"Jordyn, let me introduce you to the band." Asher looks to his right, his hand coming down onto the shoulder of the bandmate sitting next to him, "This here is Dean, our drummer. Next to him is Zayden, he plays guitar, along with Noah who is sitting next to him, he is our bass guitarist. Jesse is piano and keyboard and last one there next to you is Dawson."

"It's nice to meet everyone." I look to each and smile.

CHAPTER FOUR

ASHER

I have to admit, I'm tempted to make Dawson get up and trade seats with me. I feel a slight stab of envy knowing he gets to sit so close to her.

When Jordyn walked up to the table it took everything I had not to get up and meet her at the chair. She had changed into a dress with a jean jacket, her long hair was down, and her blue eyes looked like they were going to pop out of her head when she saw that the whole band was here. She recovered quickly, if I wasn't paying attention I would have missed the excitement that flashed though her eyes.

The waiter stops at our table and Jordyn looks up at him to give him her drink order. I'm hoping to have her attention back to me when she finishes but instead Steven decides to start up a conversation with her.

"I'm not sure how to ask this but I'm going to go ahead and just ask. How do we go about communicating with you, Jordyn?" Steven asks, and I think for the first time I see him flush a little with embarrassment.

I'm waiting for Sean to translate, but he has no need to, she is the one to answer, "I have mastered lip reading pretty well. As long as I'm looking at you I can usually figure out what you are saying. Mr. Emly will sign for me tonight, to make sure I don't misunderstand anything."

Her hands move as she speaks and I find it fascinating to watch.

"She is deaf?" Dean leans over to me and asks, I can hear the disbelief in his voice.

"Trust me, I was just as shocked earlier today, but wait until you hear her sing."

"Jordyn," Steven's voice brings my attention back to the conversation between Jordyn and himself. I want to learn everything I can about her. "I know Scott has already offered you a place in the band, which tells me a lot about you. I did listen to your track today that was recorded, I think I agree with him completely when he says you will be a great addition for the band."

Sean is signing next to her as Steven speaks and I watch her bounce back and forth between the two men as Steven talks to her.

"I appreciate you guys saying that," her voice is smooth, but her cheeks have turned a little red with the compliments.

"With that being said, I'd like to offer a contract to you and have you sign on with the band," Scott is the next to speak.

Jordyn's eyes work around the table as though she is

looking for some sign that someone isn't in agreement with Steven and Scott's opinion.

"Can I ask one question?" Her eyes come upon me.

"Ask anything," I answer.

"You guys are at the top of the charts right now. Why are you looking at bringing in another member, and why a woman?"

"I'll be honest with you, this is completely Scott's idea. I didn't think we needed any new members, regardless of their gender, but he thinks a woman's touch will drive us over the top." I'm going to be forward with her and honest.

"So you don't agree with bringing me into the group?" she questions.

"I showed up today to humor Scott, then you sang, and I was taken by your voice. I agree with Scott, I think you will be a great addition to our band."

She looks around the table to the rest of the guys in the band, "What do you guys think?"

I'm finding myself a little more impressed by her. She isn't going to make this decision without knowing how the band feels. Most people would jump on the train of popularity and fame without caring what anyone thinks, not Jordyn.

The five guys look between each other, Zayden is the one to answer her question. "You asking our opinion says a lot about you, Jordyn. I'm not going to say I'm not curious on how this is going to work. You can't hear."

Zayden is our most outspoken bandmate. He says it as he sees it, and if you don't like it, that is your problem.

Jordyn laughs, "Yes, Zayden, I'm deaf," she looks over at Sean, "this amazing man right here has taught me how to feel the music. I haven't always been deaf, I think that helps out a little as well."

That explains how her speech is so clear, now my interest in her story has piqued. What caused her to lose her hearing?

"I'm not going to say there won't be a few moments of hiccups while I try to adapt to you guys and you to me, but I promise I'll do everything I can to keep things normal for everyone."

"I have an idea," Scott speaks up. "Why don't we bring the band into the studio on Monday? We hit out a couple of the songs. That gives Jordyn the weekend to get familiar with the songs. We record, you guys decide."

"I think that sounds like a great idea," Steven agrees.

"Maybe we can get together and work on a couple of the songs before Monday," I hear myself suggest.

Sean translates because she wasn't looking at me when I made my suggestion. Her head whips around and her eyes are large with shock.

"I think it would be good for the two of us to go over a couple of the songs," I suggest once again, as she quickly recovers from the shock.

"Um, sure, I would like that."

"I'm sure she would," my brother's voice comes from down the table.

"Shut up, Noah," I shoot my brother a warning look, her eyes follow mine down to my brother.

She laughs and the sound flows through the room. I find myself shifting in my chair slightly as my jeans become a little tighter. My eyes meet my brother's again and the smug, knowing smile he is giving me makes me want to punch him.

Dinner flows from there. Most of Jordyn's attention is between Scott, Sean and Steven as they talk business. The guys all talk amongst themselves and me, well, I can't seem to keep my eyes off the woman across from me. Every once in while I catch her side glancing at me and then watch as her cheeks brighten up when she notices me catching her stealing a glance.

I can't imagine a world where I couldn't listen to music. It soothes me when I'm stressed, it cheers me up when I'm upset. It's a mainstream of my life, what would I do if my life was surrounded by silence? Yet, here is a perfect example of someone not giving up on what they love and finding a new way to cope. I envy her for that, but not sure I would have been able to do the same, especially if I was given a taste of it only to have it taken away from me.

Walking out of the restaurant, I'm watching as she says goodbye to everyone. Sean taps her on the shoulder, "How about I walk you to your car?"

This is my chance, a little alone time with her. "Um, Sean, I can walk her over to her car," I offer.

Sean looks over at Jordyn with the question in his eyes, and she nods. Holding out my hand to Sean, I shake his, "I promise she will get to the car safe. It was nice to meet you today, I'm sure we will see each other again soon."

"Nice to finally meet you as well. Scott talks about you guys all of the time. Have a nice evening." He signs something to Jordyn and she laughs.

We both watch a moment as the rest of the group

heads in different directions toward their parked cars. "All right, are you going to tell me what he said?"

With smiling eyes, she looks up at me and just shakes her head no. It's like telling secrets, loudly, right in front of the person.

"Fine, lead the way."

"So you didn't want to add a member?" Her question surprises me.

"I didn't see why we needed another member, but Scott, when he gets an idea he runs with it and there is no stopping him."

"How long has the band been together?"

"Most of us since high school. Dawson joined us after we signed on with Scott. He picks up on the percussions.

We walk up to a four-door Jeep and she stops, I find myself disappointed that we have reached her car.

"I need your number so we can set up a time this weekend to meet up and work on songs, if you are still good with it?" I ask.

"I know you are probably busy this weekend, you don't have to, I understand."

"Actually I have no plans." I'm not leaving without her number and knowing we get to meet up this weekend. Reaching into my pocket, I pull my phone out and unlock the screen. Starting a new contact, I hand it to her.

She doesn't hesitant in taking it. After putting her number in she hands it back and turns to open the door to her Jeep.

"I'll call you tomorrow, if that's all right?"

Once in her seat, she reaches over to grab the door. I stop her from shutting it, "No answer?"

"To what?" For the first time her hands come up and she signs as she talks.

I want to smack myself, she can't hear me. "I asked if it's all right that I call you tomorrow?"

"Here is your first lesson on calling someone who is deaf," she is laughing a little and it takes everything in me not to pull her to me and claim those lips, "don't!"

"I'm sorry?" I ask confused.

"Asher, I can't hear, calling me won't work. You have to text or face time."

"Got it, we have a comedian here."

She shakes her head, "No, just a friendly reminder."

I'm not going to admit to her that I would have probably tried calling tomorrow instead of texting. She would have seen the missed call and I would have looked like an ass. If anything her little humor now is saving me from a very embarrassing moment tomorrow.

"I'll text."

She smiles and starts up her vehicle. That's my clue, I take a step back and shut her door for her and watch as she pulls out of the parking lot.

"Can we go now? I mean, that is if you are done daydreaming." My brother's voice comes from behind me.

"You are going to get yourself punched one of these days." My truck is parked two spots back and my brother is standing there leaning against the passenger side, laughing.

We drove in tonight together, but right now I'm very tempted to leave him here.

CHAPTER FIVE

JORDYN

Pulling out of the parking lot I glance back in my rearview mirror, Asher is still standing there watching me as I drive away. I just gave my number to Asher James. I'm waiting for myself to wake up and realize today was just a dream. Pulling over to the side of the road, I pull out my phone and send a quick text to Megan.

Me: On my way home, meet me there, have so much to tell you.

The response is instant.

Megan: On my way.

She lives in the same apartment complex just a few buildings over, so she is there and waiting in front of my door when I walk up.

"No tears, a wide smile, I'm going to say it went good with the producer today," she signs as I walk up.

"You won't believe what happened to me today."

Walking inside, I throw my phone onto the table and hang my jacket on the back of one of the dining chairs.

Plopping down on the couch, I rest my head back, taking my first deep, steady breath all day. What a day!

"Spill it. Am I going to have a famous friend? Are they signing you to an album deal?" Her hands are flying in front of me and her lips are moving just as fast.

"So let me start with telling you, the producer friend of Mr. Emly's happens to be Scott Trival."

Megan gives me a blank stare, she has no idea who I'm talking about.

"All right, so Scott Trival is the music producer and manager for the band Driven Roads."

Her eyes go wide, she knows them. "Wow, Mr. Emly has some important friends."

"I'm standing in the sound room, getting ready to start, when you won't believe who walks through the door."

"Jordyn, I love the suspense in this story, but I've waited all day to hear what has happened. Can we just cut to the good stuff? I see the excitement radiating all over you, so I know this is good."

Megan can't be described as patient. She is terrible to go watch a movie with, she just wants to see the end without all the good stuff in the middle. Surprises have never been her thing, and patience, well, there isn't any.

"Asher James came into the studio today."

"Asher James! You mean, Asher James, lead singer of Driven Roads? That Asher James?" She sits down on the coffee table in front of me, her hands on my knees, shaking them, "Come on, what happened?"

"I sang, he sang along with me. They liked it. I've been asked to join the group." I shorten the story for my friend.

"Wait, what?" She sits up straight and shock spreads across her face.

"I have been asked to join Driven Roads," I repeat myself. It's sounds unbelievable to me as well and I was there.

Grabbing my hand, she stands, pulling me up with her. "You are joining the band Driven Roads? Jordyn, do you know how big that is? They are blowing the charts up right now."

"Megs, I know who they are. I'm already a nervous wreck. I'm supposed to record with the band on Monday and make my final decision."

"Final decision, you mean you haven't told them yes already?" Her hands are flying all over the place, no words, just exasperation.

"We all agreed tonight at dinner to start there first."

"You had dinner with the whole band tonight?"

"Yes and..." I'm not sure how she is going to respond when I tell her Asher and I are getting together this weekend. These are the moments not being able to hear isn't so bad.

"And..." she pushes for me to go on.

"Asher asked for my number. We are getting together this weekend to work on a couple of the songs before Monday."

She is pacing the room and talking to herself, I'm going to assume to herself, no one else is here and she isn't looking at me. Finally, she plops down in the recliner.

"You have had one hell of a day, my friend." She looks over at me puzzled, "How are you staying so calm?"

"Calm? No, there hasn't been a moment of calmness

since I walked into the studio this morning. Trust me, my head has been spinning all day. I didn't want to say anything earlier until I was sure. My parents don't even know yet. I wanted to make sure before I said anything."

"You understand what all of this means, right?"

Sitting down onto the couch once again, I lean back and take another deep breath. Do I know what this means? The question runs over and over again in my brain. "It means my life is about to get interesting."

"Interesting! Your life is about to do a complete one-eighty, my friend. You are used to quiet and calm. This is going to be everything but calm, although quiet you kind of have in spades."

Picking up a pillow, I throw it at her, "Thanks."

Grabbing the pillow, she gets up and comes to sit down next to me. Taking my hand, she looks right at me. "I'm so happy for you, Jordyn. This is something you have dreamed about since I can remember, even before the accident, and you have worked so hard to keep that dream alive since your accident. You are going to be great."

"Thanks, Megs." Placing my head on her shoulder, I realize how lucky I am to have her in my life. She has pushed me more than anyone to keep moving forward with my dreams of becoming a singer.

"I can't believe I gave Asher James my number today," I look up at her.

"That man is hot, I have no idea how you can sing with him and not fall into those baby blues of his. I know members of that band as single, don't forget your friend."

"Trust me, I won't be leaving you behind. I'm going to need you right there with me through all of this."

"You mean I have to hang out with a bunch of fine guys? I think I can do that."

"You know they say you know who your true friends are once you hit it big? I have a feeling I'm going to be used a little," I tease her.

Her hand comes up, her finger and thumb spaced slightly apart, "Just a little."

Sitting up, I grab the pillow next to me and swing it, smacking her across the arm with it, "Thanks, best friend."

Sunday morning, and once again I find myself looking at my phone. Maybe Asher changed his mind about meeting up this weekend. Maybe he was just being nice. He made the comment in front of everyone at the table, asking for my number when he walked me to my car, maybe he figured he should ask to be nice. He didn't offer his number so that I could text him. I'm not going to lie, it hurts a little. I was excited and probably read more into it than I should have. He said he wasn't busy this weekend, but the man is a huge celebrity, I'm sure if he has a weekend free he doesn't want to spend it with some girl he doesn't know.

He did mention he didn't understand why Scott thought they needed anyone added to the group, I just wish he would have been more forward with me.

My phone vibrates against my hand and I about throw it across the room with surprise and excitement. Juggling it a bit to turn it around to open the screen up, I take a deep breath and tell myself to calm down.

Megan: Any word yet?

Damn, it's Megan, not Asher. She has been texting at least once an hour since yesterday morning. Now I wish I never said anything to her, if he doesn't text then I'm going to look like the fool.

Me: Nope!

This is crazy. I can't sit here and wait for him to text. I downloaded the words to all of the group's songs last night and I need to make sure I have them all down before tomorrow. Today I'm going to run through them and make sure I'm ready for tomorrow's meeting and recording session.

Again my phone vibrates, I'm not even sure I want to look at it. Megan would only be trying to help, but she would be telling me he isn't that big of a deal and to not worry, which we both know is a crock of crap. Or she will be trying to tell me she will tell him off when she meets him, but we both know the moment she came face to face with a hot country singer she would be all fan girl toward him.

Again it vibrates, and then again.

Picking it up off the couch, I figure I better respond before she decides to walk over here. I love her, but really don't want anyone over today. Right now, all I want to do is work on the songs.

Swiping the screen, I find a number that isn't saved into my phone.

555-4125: Jordyn, is this your number?

555-4125: Please tell me this is you!

555-4125: The other number belongs to a seventy-one-year-old woman, who doesn't sing.

Wait, what? Why is this person talking about a

seventy-one-year-old woman who can't sing? I'm going to assume this is Asher, maybe...

Me: Who is this?

I send back. I'm pretty sure this is Asher, but he hasn't told me yet.

555-4125: Nope, not going there again. I need to know if this is Jordyn first.

I'm thinking there is a pretty good story here, and I'm almost positive this is Asher.

555-4125: Sean gave me this number.

The text comes through before I can respond to the one before it. If Mr. Emly gave him my number then I am going to bet it's Asher. He wouldn't just fling my number around to just anyone.

Me: Yes, this is Jordyn.

I wait as I watch the three little dots continuously roll at the bottom of the screen letting me know he is writing back. Now I'm more curious than ever to know the story about the woman.

555-4125: Are you sure?

Me: Yes!

555-4125: O.K., so I'm going to call this number right now so we can talk.

I'm puzzled, why would he call? He knows I can't talk to him on the phone. I get this is all new to him, but I'm sure he remembers that part. Then it hits me, he is making sure this is me.

Me: No, calling wouldn't do you any good, I wouldn't be able to hear a word you said.

Asher: Perfect, it is you. This is Asher.

Laughing, I take a deep breath, and realize how

excited I am that he actually reached out. Then it hits me, I put my number into his phone, did I give him the wrong number? I must have, how else would he have called the wrong person?

Me: I think I need to apologize. I'm assuming I hit in the wrong number when I put my number in your phone.

Asher: At first I was thinking you may have done it on purpose, but I wasn't willing to give up, so I called Scott to get Sean's number so that I could get your number. Yesterday, I had a very interesting conversation with a very feisty grandmother.

He has hunted down my number. Instead of thinking I was just blowing him off, wait... Who would blow off Asher James?

Me: What makes you think I didn't give you the wrong number on purpose?

I'm not sure what has gotten into me, who plays this kind of game with one of the hottest men in country music? I watch for his response, but nothing. Maybe I've gone a little too far.

CHAPTER SIX

I read her text and think for a moment. She has a good point, how do I know she didn't give me the wrong number on purpose? I'm not sure how to respond without sounding conceited and completely full of myself. I'm going with humble, but before I can respond I get another text from her.

Jordyn: Asher, I'm kidding.

There is that sense of humor again. She pulled a little of it out at dinner the other night. Good to know. One thing about texting, you can't tell if a person's tone is playful or serious. You just interpret it as best you can. Then add in only having met the person once and the conversation can take all kinds of turns.

Me: Good, because I didn't want to have to call back grandma and ask her to come sing with me again.

Jordyn: Sounds like an interesting story.

Interesting isn't the word I would have used to

describe my day yesterday and the conversations I had with a woman that I at first thought was Jordyn.

Me: Let's just put it this way, I should have known the second the woman called me it wasn't you. I'll tell you the story when you get here.

Jordyn: So you are still inviting me over after I made you hunt down my number?

I'm not sure how forward I can be with her yet. I would have given away a whole concert full of tickets to get her number.

Me: I'm just going to take it as an honest mistake.

Jordyn: You do that

She types back instantly and I find myself wondering again. Enough with the texting. Typing out my address, I send it to her.

Me: How about in an hour?

There isn't much time before she responds.

Jordyn: See you then.

Leaning back against the couch, I close my eyes and her voice from the other day in the studio fills my head, like it does every time I close my eyes. The smoothness of her tone, mixing with a little rasp and grit of country but all controlled to perfection. Watching her hand tap lightly above her heart was mesmerizing.

"Are you asleep or dreaming about Jordyn again?" My brother's voice breaks through my thoughts.

"I thought you said you were leaving?"

"I'm on my way out. Don't worry, I won't be here when she gets here. Are you sure it's her, though? I mean we'll go broke if you keep giving away seats to grandmothers."

"Get out of here." I stand up and start walking him toward the door.

All the guys were here yesterday when I was on the phone with Milly, our now newest fan and grandmother of four granddaughters who all now have backstage passes to our next hometown concert. If you want to be mercifully teased by your bandmates and brother, you have them around when you find out a girl gave you the wrong number.

Noah had a couple of beers yesterday and decided to stay the night, but it is by far time for him to go home, before I pick him up and throw him out of my house.

"Maybe I should stay, I'm not sure if I believe Jordyn is actually coming over. You may be wanting to save face and just telling me this."

"I going to kick your ass, now get out of my house."

Laughing, he opens the door, "Fine, but I'm asking Jordyn tomorrow. I already like this girl."

"Leave! Now!" I shut the door on him.

I'm never going to be able to live yesterday down with the guys, but it's all right. I can handle a little teasing, in the end I found her.

The knock at my door has my heart racing a little with nerves. This is crazy, why does this woman have this kind of effect on me? Friday night at dinner I would have been all right with picking my band mate out of his chair and tossing him on the floor so that I could have his seat next to her. It took a lot of restraint not to do it.

Jogging the couple of feet to the door, I open it to see a

vision in front of me. Jordyn stands there wearing a simple pair of jeans, black shirt and boots. Nothing fancy, nothing screaming out to look at her. A natural look that takes my breath away.

"Sorry, I'm a little late."

"No problem, it's not like we had a set time." Standing off to the side, I allow room for her to enter. "Come on in."

She smiles shyly and walks in past me. "Did you have any problems finding the place?" I ask as she walks in and I shut the door behind her.

No answers. Damn it! This isn't going to be as easy as I thought. My nerves jump a little more in my chest when I realize, we may have a little trouble with communication.

"Your home is beautiful." She turns to me with a bright smile on her face.

I just nod, now feeling self-conscious. This might have been a bad idea.

"Is everything all right?" She becomes a little shy and starts to look around. Almost like she is looking for something she may have missed.

I realize she isn't signing today like she did the other day when we were all together.

"I'm realizing I'm not sure how to make this work." I find myself talking slower and louder than normal. It takes everything in me not to slap myself on the head.

"Asher, if you are uncomfortable, I understand. We don't have to do this, I can work on this alone."

Now I feel like an ass. She is communicating with me just fine, it's all me and I need to get over it. If I don't, she is going to walk out the door.

"The last thing I want is for you to leave, Jordyn. Come on," taking her hand, I lead us down the hallway and to the small studio I have set up.

Shutting the door behind us, I watch as she looks around with amazement. Her eyes are large and round as she looks between the sound board and the sound studio. Walking over to the wall, she fingers the gold record I have hanging there.

"It's amazing what this group has done in such a short time." She turns to look at me with a shy smile on her face.

"Well, it's all thanks to Scott. As soon as the dotted line was signed by all of us he was in hyper speed. There was no time to even think. It's been a wild year."

"So what did you have in mind for today?"

To have your lips would be nice, I think to myself, but refrain from voicing my thoughts. "Well, to start with I would like to understand a little more on how things work for you."

She gives me a puzzled look, "What I mean is, I'm curious. Friday in the studio, when did you know that the music was starting? You were right on beat."

Her cheeks brighten a little, "Actually, that was lots of work on the part of Mr. Emly. We worked a lot on a signal for me to know when the music started."

I think back to Friday and how her hand came up to her chest right before the song started. "Is that why you were tapping your chest?"

She nods.

"All right, but what signal did he give you?"

"He tapped his thigh when the music started. It was a

sign we worked on since I would be in the studio. I can't wear the headphones, they are kind of useless to me." She shrugs and again her cheeks brighten a little more.

My hands are itching to reach out to her, but instead I tuck them into my jean pockets. "I don't mean to hound you with a bunch of questions, but I have a few."

"It's all right, ask away. I don't mind."

"Well, really I only have one question. How do you feel the music even outside of the studio?"

She looks around the room and walks over to my guitar, but before she picks it up she looks over her shoulder at me, "Do you mind?"

Shaking my head, I signal with my hand to go ahead, "Please."

She surprises me even further when she grabs it and ask me to sit down on a stool. Placing the guitar in my hands, she asks, "Do you have ear plugs or noise cancelling headphones, or something?"

I think and then I realize what I have that might work perfectly. Handing her the guitar, I hold up a hand for her to hold on for a minute and I leave the room.

It takes me only a couple of minutes to find what I am looking for. Walking back into the studio ,I hold them up for her to see. "My brother and I grew up doing a lot of shooting with our dad, we always wear ear plugs to help with the sound."

Sitting back down, I take the guitar back from her, "What now?"

"Play a little something for me."

All right, I'm not sure where she is going with this, but

I do as she asks me to. I watch her face as I play the beginning part to our song "Road Not Taken." She lets me play for a few moments then stops me.

"All right, now I want you to put the plugs in and do the same thing."

As I put the plugs in my ears, she walks behind me. When I feel her press up against my back, I hear my own moan deep in my throat. Her not being able to hear isn't such a bad thing right this minute.

She surprises me even further when she reaches around and wraps her arms around me, one of her hands covering mine on the neck of the guitar. She taps my shoulder and points at the guitar. I'm assuming she is telling me to start playing again.

I begin the same song and realize she is pressing the guitar up against my chest as I play. I can hear very little of the sound, but what surprises me is what I feel. The vibration against my chest. I close my eyes and try to tune out the sound all together. As I change cords, I realize I can feel a slight difference in the way it vibrates against my skin. My senses start to heighten a little more, her right hand comes around and starts tapping slightly just above my heart. She is in perfect rhythm with what I am playing. I smile to myself when I feel the song through my skin. It vibrates along my chest, down my arms, and over my stomach.

Her head is right next to mine, I can feel her breath on my neck. All I need to do is turn my head and her lips would be right there. The thought is there, the temptation is harder to ignore, but before I can act, I feel Jordyn's arms fall away from around me and she steps away from my back.

Pulling the plugs from my ears, I hear her heavy breathing behind me. I have the same effect on her as she does me.

CHAPTER SEVEN

JORDYN

I was so caught up on feeling the strum of the guitar and the beat of his heart under my hand I almost forgot who I was pressing my body up against. To top everything off, my head was so close to his, my lips were basically brushing up against his ear.

Taking a couple of deep breaths, I try to calm this feeling raging through me before I trust my voice to be any kind of calm. "I'm sorry."

Asher turns, the plugs now out of his ears, and looks up at me with a puzzled expression. "Sorry about what? That was amazing. I've never felt anything like that, the sound, I guess you would call it, through my body. It makes a person appreciate the instrument all that much more. That is what you feel?"

"That is just one example. That was the first way Mr. Emly showed me to feel the sounds, with my guitar."

My nerves start to settle again, he isn't thinking of anything other than what I was trying to show him. He has no idea that all it would have taken was a slight turn of his head and our lips would be speaking a different language as well.

"So I was thinking, we should probably work on starting me off in the studio tomorrow, since once again I'm going to be without the music. I was thinking maybe we could work something out with a couple of the songs so that way there isn't a lot of confusion tomorrow, make it a little easier for everyone."

"All right, so where do we start?"

"I need your heart."

His blue eyes darken and he stands now only inches away from me. He grabs my hand and places it back onto his chest, "Show me where to start."

Before I can even anticipate his next move, his lips claim mine. Shock, that's the only reason I can't respond at first. I didn't see this coming and it happened so quickly. My hand is still pressed tightly between us right above his heart and I feel the beat of it quicken. Something falls at my feet but I don't care what it may have been, because once his other hand cups my face and neck I am lost. I find myself now kissing him back.

My hand fists around his shirt, holding on so that I don't end up on the floor when my knees give out, because they feel like they might. He doesn't make any move to take it any further, but he isn't making any move to end the kiss either, his lips find a beat of their own and he is in complete control of it. My lips, that is all he is seeking, and I'm giving him full permission to explore.

Too soon, he pulls away, instantly my eyes fly open and find his. I need to see his reaction, make sure I don't miss his words, so with that, as hard as it is, I lean back slightly, breaking the body contact between us so that I can see his whole face.

He doesn't say anything at first. I watch as his eyes bounce between my lips and my eyes. Like he is contemplating if he is going to kiss me again or not.

"I know I should apologize, but that is something I have wanted to do since I opened the door. If I'm being honest, actually since Friday."

I'm watching every movement of his lips as he is speaking, but I swear I'm not reading them right. I'd swear he just told me he has been wanting to kiss me since Friday.

"Jordyn, now that I know how those lips taste, I'm not sure I'm going to be able to stop wanting them."

With his hand at the back of my neck, he pulls me back to him, once again claiming my lips. A thought shoots between all of the haze and washes over me like a bucket of cold water being dumped right on my head. This is Asher James, most sought after man in country music by the ladies. I'm sure women switched over to country music just because of this man.

This time I'm the one to end the kiss. I push back out of his arms and out of his reach. Whatever was at my feet causes me to stumble back, looking down I see Asher's guitar. Picking it up off the ground, I lay it down on the stool, giving myself a second to catch my breath and unscramble my head. Once I think I have composure of myself, I chance a look at him.

"Asher, I'm not one of the fan girls. I didn't come here

to make out with the country star and be happy for the few hot moments with you."

Quickly, I move past him so that I can leave. Maybe this isn't going to be a great idea.

His hand shoots out, wrapping around my arm and stops me just as I move past him. He pulls at me once again and I find myself being held tight against his chest, my hand just above his heart. "I'm not that kind of guy, Jordyn."

I have to tip my head back to see his lips as he talks.

"I'm sorry if at any moment I made you feel like that."

He takes a step back and I instantly feel the cool air rush between us. He doesn't release his hold on my arm, though, his grip actually tightens as though he is scared I may leave.

"Talk to me, Jordyn."

I have no idea what to say, or what he is wanting me to say. There has been a pull between us since the first moment we sang through the glass with each other, but I just assumed it was me being a little starstruck, I mean who doesn't look at Asher James that way? There is no "star-quality" reason for him to feel that pull toward me, though.

One thing about being deaf. You learn to read people and actions because you don't have the ability to hear the tone in their voice. We look at the eyes, facial expressions, and the body language. Asher hasn't portrayed the "I'm a star" vibe to me. He seems very down to earth. I'm not seeing cocky in them either, which I find most men who think they are a gift to women tend to have pouring out of them.

"Why did you invite me over today, Asher?"

"I want to understand more about you. The moment I walked into the studio the other day something about you started pulling me in. I've never had a pull toward a woman like that before, and I'm not one to ignore what my instincts are telling me."

I'm too close to him and not understanding everything he is saying. His lips are moving very little and for the first time in a long time my disability is frustrating me. I'm already confused by his actions and not being able to fully understand what he is telling me isn't helping anything right now.

"Jordyn, don't run out on this. I didn't peg you as that kind of woman. You are strong and straightforward. The other night at dinner when you asked if the band agreed with bringing on a new member, I knew you were different. Most people who would have been handed the opportunity you are being given would have jumped and signed right away, they wouldn't have cared what anyone else thought. You asked the group what they thought, and I'm pretty sure if even one of them disapproved, you would have turned it down. Please give me that chance as well, to prove to you I'm not one of those guys either."

Deep down I know he isn't just using me for a make-out session, but I'm scared of what he is starting to make me feel.

"Asher, this may be harder than you are thinking. For example, I'm not understanding all of what you are saying and it's only confusing me. I think the mystery of how I do this is what intrigues you the most. Vibration music sends feeling through the body that most hearing people can't appreciate, it's very intimate."

Asher releases my hands and takes a couple steps back. "Jordyn," he begins and I notice he is now talking with the full motion of his lips, he is making sure I understand him, "I was taken by you the moment Sean moved to the side and I saw you standing in that sound room alone." He raises one eyebrow as if asking me if I'm understanding him.

Nodding a couple of times, I answer his unasked question, so he continues, "I didn't even know you were deaf then. I'm not going to lie to you and say that I'm not intrigued by your ability to do what you love without the most essential part of what music is about, and that is your hearing, but all that did was draw me to you more because of your strength and passion to continue to do what you love to do. You aren't here for me to help you out, you are here to help me learn to appreciate a love we both share. I think we are going to learn so much more from you than you can from any of us."

I have no words to respond with. I just stand here staring at him. I watch as he searches my face for any sign of what I may be thinking, but I'm sure my expression is as blank as my mind is right now. Or it could be wide-eyed disbelief that this conversation is even happening right now.

He closes the space between us, his arm hooking around my waist, "Jordyn, I'm going to kiss you again."

He's telling me, not asking permission, but I know he is giving me a moment to stop him if I don't want it to happen, which may be why my next action shocks me more than it probably does him.

I don't give him a chance to kiss me first, my hand, as if by its own accord, snakes up around to the back of his head, my fingers dig into his thick hair, and I bring his lips down to mine. I feel a rumble from his chest against mine as his arms tighten around me. All thoughts of regret are wiped from my mind and at this moment, as crazy as it is to admit, I'm pretty sure I just gave my heart to Asher James.

CHAPTER EIGHT

ASHER

When I told her I was going to kiss her again, I never would've guessed she would have been the one to act first. This wasn't in the plans for today when I asked her to come over. Although I have to admit that I've had to stop myself from grabbing her a couple of times since she walked in the door. I lost all will to stay away the moment she told me she needed my heart.

It was the innocent way she asked for it that did it for me. She was simply answering my question, but the way it fell from her lips made any restraint I was holding onto just disappear. The moment our lips touched, I knew I was lost.

Then there was that moment of confusion and pain in her eyes, and I would have done anything, given up everything to take that feeling away for her, to assure her that I wasn't the type of guy she was thinking I might be.

When she told me she was confused and not understanding everything I was saying, I knew I couldn't let her walk out. I had to make her understand. I'm hoping the way she is demanding my lips right now means that there is no more confusion.

Our lips part, forehead to forehead we both just stand here for a moment in silence. The only sound in the room is our breathing as we both try to catch our breath. Her hand comes up to my chest and that's when I realize something. I hear the sound filling the room of two people trying to gain control from an intensive moment, and she feels it, with the rise and fall of my chest and the rapid beat of my heart. It's amazing to have my eyes opened to so much that I was missing before.

Friday, when I found out she was deaf, it was impossible to think about how she could enjoy music and still be so passionate about something that required hearing. In this short time with her today, I've had a small amount of what she is feeling and it's changing the way I look at music.

Stepping back, I instantly feel the absence of her warmth and want to pull her back into my arms, but there is one story I've been wanting to hear about.

"I'm very curious about something, if you don't want to tell me, though, just say so."

"What is it?"

"At dinner the other night, you mentioned you haven't always been deaf. What age were you when you lost your hearing?"

She sits down on the bench and looks up at me. I see a small hint of sadness, but more than that I see her strength shining through her eyes.

"When I was ten, we were hit by a drunk driver. The

car hit into my door, my head slammed against it causing major damage to my head, the trauma resulted in me losing my hearing. The doctors told my parents they were very surprised I lived."

My hands tighten into fist as I feel the need to punch a person I have never met. "Were you the only one hurt?"

She shakes her head. "No, my dad broke his left arm, and had a few stitches across the cheek from the glass. I was sitting behind him. My mom had some cuts from glass, my older brother, Justin, came out of the accident with no injuries."

I notice she is rubbing the side of her head, just above her left ear.

"I'm sorry, I don't mean to be nosy, I was just wondering."

Her hand stops and she removes her fingers from being buried in her hair. "Sorry, it's an impulse I think. When I'm talking about the accident it's like I can feel the throbbing all over again. I had ten staples in the side of my head, two broken ribs and a broken ankle."

I want to pull her back into my arms, comfort her from the memories I see flashing through her mind. "Can I ask you one more question?"

"Asher, you can ask anything. If I'm going to be part of this group, you should know me just as well as any other band member."

"You are nothing like the other band members."

"I'm sorry, I didn't understand that last part."

I said it more under my breath, but the slight movement of my lips must have made her think I was speaking to her. It doesn't matter if I scream or whisper, as long as my lips are moving she is going to pay attention to what is being said. That is something I'm going to have to remember.

"I do have one more question."

"Sure, what is it?"

"When you woke up, what was it like? You were so young, did you really know what was happening?"

I watch as she thinks back to that day. It's almost like the memory flashes across her eyes.

"It's hard to explain really. I remember looking around the room. I saw my mom's lips moving and saw her tears, but I couldn't understand why she was moving her mouth, but not saying anything. I remember thinking, she must have been crying so hard, she couldn't get the words out. When the doctor came in and I saw his mouth moving I knew right away something was wrong. The strangest thing is, I could hear the sound of the glass shattering around me in the car and hear my mom's screams in my head, as a memory of course. I had nightmares for weeks with the same thing over and over. About not being able to hear. My parents would be in my room, shaking me, trying to wake me up and I would think it was just the shake of the car in my dreams."

"Do you still have nightmares?"

"No, not really. Every once in a while I have one, but since I'm older I think I'm able to work through them a little better. I didn't want those sounds to be the ones I remembered and filled my head. I remember lying in my bed and remembering songs that I would listen to before the accident. I would close my eyes and try to pick apart the sounds of all of the instruments and try to remember what they sounded like. I've played the guitar since I was seven. That was the sound I missed the most. I think that's why Mr. Emly taught me to feel the guitar first, it was the instrument I was connected to the most."

"What happened to the guy that hit you?"

"He didn't make it."

The sadness in her eyes says so much about her. She is sad for the guy who lost his life, because he made a poor decision and almost caused her to lose her life. She shows no anger, which I'm not sure I could do the same. She may be alive, but he took something from her.

"He was twenty-three, my parents found out later in the report that he was coming home from a party. He was the only one in the car, which was a good thing. The only thing that saved my life was my seatbelt didn't lock up and I was pushed basically into my brother's lap."

Squatting down in front of her, I take her hands into mine. "What's it like to not hear anything?"

She shrugs. "People ask me that all of the time. It's hard to explain. It can be very lonely. You can be in a room full of people, standing back and watching all of the conversations going on around you, but it's like watching a silent movie."

"One day you'll have to try and show me."

She smiles and it takes every fiber of my being not to pull her back into my arms so that I can kiss her again, but she speaks up before I can.

"I would really like to work on a few songs before

tomorrow, if you don't mind. I'm nervous enough already, to be a little prepared will help."

Standing up, I pull her up from the bench with me, leading the way into the sound studio. "Tell me what you need me to do."

CHAPTER NINE

JORDYN

"Actually we need the music and it needs to be loud."

His eyebrow arches up in question as he watches me start to take off my shoes. "Making yourself comfortable, I like that."

Realizing how comfortable I feel around Asher is a little scary. It's happening very quickly.

"I can feel the vibration through the floor, it helps with finding the beat and keeping it."

"So you are saying, you are going to be barefoot every night in concert?"

I laugh at his questioning look, "What if I was?"

"Whatever works, I can see the questions during interviews flying at you about it, though."

"This is going to help while I learn the song's beat. Once I get it down, I'm pretty good at keeping it, with my shoes on."

"All right, where do we start?"

"Which song would you suggest we start with?"

"Well, you know 'Roads Taken,' so let's see, which one should we go with?"

I watch as he thinks about a song selection. He is pushing buttons on the sound board, I'm thinking he is going through the band's songs. I understand how life can change in a matter of moments. Good or bad, you never know what is going to happen to shift your life. In the matter of time it takes to sing one song, my life has once again shifted. I'm going from helping out with a high school choir to being a member of a famous band.

"Maybe this will be easier if I know what songs you know the words to."

My cheeks start to heat up. "All of them."

"You know all of the words to all of our songs? A fan, are you?"

"I kind of have to memorize lyrics to sing them. Not like I can sing along with the song on the radio."

He stares at me for a moment, I can't read a thing from his expression and I find myself shifting back and forth as he watches me.

"I'm trying to imagine what it's like for you. You can't just turn the radio on in the car and hear the music, sing along as you drive. The world of music is so different for you. I'm starting to understand how much we in the hearing world take advantage of sound."

I have no response. It's true, but I'm a little luckier than those who have never had the chance to hear the sounds of the world. Yes, the older I get I fear the memories I hold will fade away or that I won't remember them the right way, but I'm happy I had ten years of sound.

He looks down at my bare feet, "Shoes are off, and I

think I have a song. We can start with 'It's For Me,' now tell me what we need to do next."

"Easiest way for this to happen without being here all day on one song, it might be easier for you to start the song and for us to work me into it. Following off you is going to be easier than me starting it with you."

Closing the space between us, I place my hand on his chest, just above his heart. Taking his hand in my other hand, I bring it up and place his hand over mine.

"Find the beat, I will follow you. Start singing, I will follow in. For tomorrow we will make it simple. If it all works out we can get more detailed later."

"What do you mean, if it works out?"

"No contracts have been signed, Asher, it's kind of the purpose of tomorrow. The guys may not like this idea, you may think it's a lot of work and not worth it..."

"Just so that I'm very clear," he interrupts me before I can finish, "this is happening, Jordyn. Do you feel that beat?"

He' presses my hand harder into his chest, and I nod.

"That beat belongs to you now."

Wait, what? I try to pull my hand away, but he only tightens his hold on me.

"From the moment you knocked over the stool in the sound room the other day, there has been something pulling me to you. Then you sang, and something twisted in my chest. I can't really explain what it is, but this pull between us I don't plan to ignore."

"The other guys might not feel the same way."

"They better not feel the same way, I don't want to have to beat the shit out of my bandmates, but I will."

I can't help but laugh. "That's not what I meant, Asher." With watching his mouth, I find I get distracted by his lips very easily, especially when he is being playful. "We don't seem to be getting a lot of work done."

"That's your fault, you keep distracting me."

His lips quickly find mine before I can respond and that's when I realize, I'm probably going to be winging it quite a bit tomorrow because we are getting absolutely nothing done today, not that I'm complaining.

It took a couple of hours, but we did manage to get through a couple of the songs. I'm not really sure I can say I feel ready for tomorrow, but I'll make it work. He ordered a pizza and we made it through another song as we ate our dinner. I ended up leaving his house around eight.

Now as I'm driving home, the day's events are flying through my head, well, all of the kissing parts of it anyway. After the first kiss, I was thinking it was just a moment and was trying not to think too much of it. Then it happened again and again. Not only that, but he also mentioned a couple of times about me stealing his heart beat. I'm trying not to read too much into all of it, I could be interpreting it completely wrong. One of those 'too good to be true' moments.

The smile on my face vanishes the moment I pull into my parking spot, next to my brother's truck. He's sitting on the tailgate, not looking very happy.

My curiosity has me quickly getting out of my Jeep, "Justin, what are you doing here? Is everything all right?"

"I don't know, Jordyn." His hands are flying along with his mouth, his isn't happy. "Where have you been all day?"

"Excuse me?"

Justin and I have always been close, but after the accident he became my protector. I'll never forget the day when he told me he thought he was holding his dead sister in his arms that night. The paramedics, I was told, had a very hard time getting him to release me. He wanted to ride along with me in the ambulance and they wouldn't let him. He ran after the ambulance when it pulled away from the accident and one of the police officers had to chase after him to stop him. There is no one I love more in this world than my brother, but as we've become adults it's been hard to get him to back off a little.

"Everyone has tried getting ahold of you, Jordyn. You haven't responded to anyone. All we know is what Megan told us, and that was you went to some singer's house to work on songs."

"Some singer, really, Justin? Asher James isn't just some singer."

"I know who Asher James is, Jordyn, that's not the point. None of us know this guy, you don't know this guy. Mom and Dad have tried getting ahold of you. Megan has texted you, I have no idea how many times I've texted you today. How many of those have you answered? None! Have you even checked your phone today?"

Pulling out my phone, I see that I have fifteen text messages waiting for me to open.

"Mom and Dad knew what I was doing today and so did Megan. Heck, I even chatted with your wife before I headed over to Asher's today. Why are you acting like I'm sneaking around or something?"

"Jordyn, I get it Asher is some famous guy and all, but when you don't answer text messages from multiple people, and none of us know this guy, worrying starts to set in."

As my brother is giving me the second degree, I text my mom and apologize if I worried her. Her response doesn't surprise me much. Justin was the one worried.

"I'm sorry, Justin, I didn't mean to worry you. We were working on songs. I should have paid more attention. Now why didn't you bring my niece with you?"

"Because I had no idea how long I'd be sitting here before I was going to have to send out a search party."

"I do believe you are overreacting, but I promise you, I'll pay better attention to my phone next time."

He pushes himself off the bed of the truck to stand in front of me and wraps me in a big hug. I love my brother, and yes, I believe he is way overprotective of me, but it just makes me love him that much more.

I can never understand what he went through that night. He was the only one not injured in the accident. He watched everything from the sideline as everyone around him hustled to help my parents and myself.

Setting me back from him, I watch as his hands move. "So, how did today go?"

"It's all a little overwhelming, but exciting. I'll be able to tell you more after tomorrow."

"Are you sure you are ready for something this big?"

"All I have ever wanted to do was sing. This is quick,

I'll admit that, but exactly what I've wanted, so I'm as ready as I can be."

I see the worry in his eyes. My brother isn't a small guy, six foot, eight inches tall and nothing but muscle. He works for a security company that provides security for some very big names.

"Well, maybe I should become your bodyguard."

"Let's see if I actually sign with the band tomorrow first, before we worry about my bodyguards."

I haven't gotten much sleep. The words to the songs kept flashing through my mind, along with the make-out sessions with the lead singer of the band. At some point around three or four this morning I was finally able to convince my brain it was time to shut down and get a little sleep. When I say little, it means I was awake at six this morning.

Pulling into the parking lot of the studio, I sit here for a moment and just take everything in. My life is about to change drastically. If today works out, I'll be signing contracts to join as the new member of Driven Roads. I've dreamt of a moment like this since I was a little girl. Today would be perfect if Mr. Emly was able to be here. He wasn't very informative on why he couldn't make it, but he did send me a text first thing this morning telling me he knew I'd be great and to remember to breathe and just enjoy the feeling of the beat.

Megan offered to join me today, as my "interpreter," but I gently turned down the offer. I know she loves me and all but it had nothing to do with helping me communicate, and all to do with the guys of the band. Plus, if this is going to work, we need to be able to communicate without me always having an interpreter around. The point of today is to see if I am going to be able to flow into a position as a new member of this group, everything has to work to do that. At least that was the argument I used with Megan.

The clock on my dashboard reminds me that if I don't get inside I won't be setting a great first impression. Taking one last deep breath, I grab my bag from the passenger seat and just as I'm about to open my door, it's opened for me.

Jumping, I turn to find Asher standing there. "Sorry, I didn't mean to scare you."

Willing my heart back into my chest, I wave it off. "It's fine, just surprised me is all. Am I that late?"

"No, you aren't late at all. I just thought I'd wait and walk in with you."

Stepping down out of my Jeep, Asher surprises me when he pins me up against the side of my vehicle and closes the space between us, his lips finding mine. My body molds to his, my bag falls from my hand to the ground unnoticed as my arms come up around his shoulders and my fingers bury into the hair at the back of his head. The kiss is demanding and my body hums with a need.

CHAPTER TEN

ASHER

With her fingers buried into my hair and her body relaxed against mine, giving me full rein of her lips, it is hard to think. We are standing in the middle of the parking lot, anyone can see us, but right now all that matters is this woman's lips on mine. We need to get inside, but I can't seem to pull myself away from her.

Jordyn is the one to end the kiss. "I think we should go inside."

As I try to calm the flood of liquid fire raging through my body, all I can do is nod my acknowledgment of her words, but I'm not ready to put space between us.

"Asher, what is everyone going to think if we are late and walk in together?"

"Personally, I don't give a damn what they think, but I'm sure they can understand my needs. I haven't kept my attraction to you a secret from anyone. This weekend, I was the center of many jokes after my call with a grandmother."

"Yes, a story you have yet to tell me. We never got to that yesterday."

No, instead I was becoming very familiar with this woman's lips.

"Trust me, I'm sure the guys will have plenty of jokes about it today. If you just piece it all together you will find the same humor in the situation as they did."

"Well then, let's get going, this is a story I'm very interested to know about." She bends down to pick up her discarded bag and moves to shut the door to her Jeep.

"Even at the expense of my humility?"

"Something tells me you aren't so easy to embarrass."

She is going to fit into this group just fine.

Leaning in for one more kiss, I take her hand and we head to the studio and into the firing zone. I know once we walk in, the guys are going to have plenty to say. All directed at me, of course.

Walking down the hallway to the studio, Jordyn's hand tightens around mine. I like that she finds security in my touch. Stopping at the door, I take a moment. She looks calm and ready, but I feel the slight shake in her hand.

Turning to her, I make sure I have her full attention. "Hey, this isn't an audition."

"I never knew I was auditioning in the first place. Mr. Emly kind of tricked me into this. I asked for today because I want to make sure it's a good fit for everyone involved, but it's all still a little nerve-racking."

Wrapping my arm around her waist, I pull her up tight against me, "Perfect fit."

Smacking me on the chest, she says, "That's not what I'm talking about."

"So are these..." I claim her lips.

"This better not be Milly, or we are kicking you out of the band." Zayden's voice comes from behind me. I hadn't even heard the door to the studio open.

"Trust me, not Milly."

Jordyn looks between Zayden and myself. Her cheeks are a little flushed, but she is bouncing a puzzled look between the two of us. I have to keep reminding myself she can't hear.

"Zayden here thinks he is funny. He thought you may be Milly, the grandmother from the other day and our newest fan." I explain the situation.

"Not 'our,' all she wants is you, man!"

I hear a quiet laugh escape from Jordyn. Turning my attention to her, I remind her, "This is all your fault, don't forget that."

"How is this my fault?"

"If you wouldn't have given me the wrong number to begin with, none of this would be happening."

"Yes, but where would the fun have been in that?"

Her quick response has Zayden laughing. "I'm going to like having her around."

"He doesn't need any help or encouragement."

"I didn't hear a thing. I have no idea what you mean." She smiles up at me and I want nothing more than to shut the door to the studio, leaving all of them to think what they want and take her back to my place.

With her hand still in mine, I turn and push past

Zayden, who is holding open the door, and lead the two of us into the studio.

"I'm Zayden, the funny one," I hear my friend introduce himself to Jordyn as we pass by him.

"Zayden, I believe you are the one to tell me the story of Milly then. I can't wait to hear what exactly happened."

"I am actually looking forward to meeting the woman. She played him along for some time through text. The best part was when she called..."

"I think we can leave the story of Milly for another time," I interrupt Zayden's storytelling.

My brother gets up and walks over to Jordyn, his hand extended. "I'm Noah, his brother. The excitement in his eyes when his phone rang was one thing," he continues on with Zayden's story, "but the confusion that quickly followed, now that was priceless. It's like his brain finally caught up, why would the deaf girl be calling?"

There it was, the only part of that whole damn situation that I was hoping she wouldn't be told. The night at the restaurant she had made it clear to me that calling wasn't the best option when you were trying to reach a deaf person. Jordyn has this damn effect on me making me feel like I'm back in high school and my first crush is finally noticing I'm alive. My head gets all twisted around and nothing comes out right the first time she talks to me.

Dawson is up next, as he extends his hand out to Jordyn. "I'm Dawson. That little old lady belted out her best attempt of a song none of us knew the moment Asher said hello. We weren't even on speakerphone and all of us could hear every out-of-tune note her dear heart sang."

"Wait," Jordyn puts up a hand to stop Dawson, "I

want to make sure I'm understanding. You mean she actually called to sing?"

Jordyn's laugh has me all twisted up inside. I don't care that each of the guys are taking their turn in embarrassing me, to hear her laugh I'll take the brunt of whatever they dish out with their storytelling. She seems very relaxed and her full attention is on whatever they are saying.

"I'm thinking we need to invite her up during our concert and have the two of them sing. Dean." Our drummer and my best friend since elementary school chimes in with his introduction.

I watch as Jordyn turns her attention to Jesse, the only one who hasn't told his part of the story. He stretches out his hand to her, "It's nice to see you again, Jordyn. I'm Jesse and I wasn't there to even end this story for you. I was at home with my little girl. Mommy needed a girls' night out."

Tapping Jordyn on the shoulder, I bring her attention back to me. "Jesse is the only guy here who is married. Dawson has a girlfriend. The rest are in the 'play stage' of their love lives."

"And you?"

"I'm working on it."

Her one eyebrow lifts in question. "Working on what?"

"I don't play, Jordyn. I'm looking for the real thing."

Her cheeks turn a slight shade of red and she looks around to see the reaction from the guys.

Taking her chin in my hand, I bring her eyes back to me. "I told you, I'm not hiding this from anyone."

She nods slightly and a small smile curves her lips. I can't help myself from leaning forward and placing a quick kiss on the corner of that smile.

"All right, come on, guys. We need to get moving on this. I only booked out the studio for a couple hours. We have songs to sing and contracts to sign," Scott announces to the room.

Jordyn gives me a puzzled look. "He is ready for us to get started." I give her the short recap.

Movement in the room has Jordyn looking in every direction. At this moment I wish Sean would have been able to join. None of us know sign language. He isn't always going to be around, though, and together as a group we are going to have to learn to adapt, all of us.

Squeezing her hand that I haven't released since the parking lot, I bring her attention to me. "Relax. I'll make sure you aren't left behind."

I watch her shoulders relax a little and she nods. Leading the way, I walk into the sound studio and point for her to take a seat on one of the stools. While everyone gets set up, I motion to her that I'll be right back.

Leaving her in the room, I go back out and talk with Scott for a moment. "We all need to remember, if she isn't looking at you she has no idea you are talking. I was hoping Sean would join us today."

I notice a change in his facial expression at the mention of Sean, but he recovers it quickly. Fast enough that I'm not sure if it's something I should question or ignore.

"There are going to be some adjusting, Ash, but it will be fine. You seem more concerned about it than her.

Relax, she is all right. If she has questions, she will ask. I spoke to Sean this morning, he fully believes she will adapt just fine. Don't smother her. I see what's happening between the two of you and I can't say that I blame you, but she is very independent, you need to be there beside her, not always trying to make things easier for her."

"She's nervous." I make an excuse for my behavior.

"Of course she is, I'd be worried if she wasn't. I'm just saying, let her walk on her own two feet. She will speak up if she needs to. Being protective is one thing, coddling is another. She doesn't seem to be the type of woman who needs to be coddled."

I suddenly feel embarrassed myself. I'm thankful my back is to Jordyn and that only Scott and I can hear this conversation. He is right. I'm taking Jordyn's nerves and becoming way overprotective of her. She is strong and has no problem voicing what's on her mind. It's me that is having more of an issue with her deafness than her. If she was that worried today, I'm sure she would have arranged for someone to join us.

Scott places a hand on my shoulder, very fatherly like, and steps in a little closer to me. "Asher, like anyone without disabilities, it takes a little time to get used to them. Sometimes it's harder for those who don't have it, than those with it. You like her, that is very obvious, just relax. She may stumble a little and that's all right."

"Thanks, Scott."

"Now let's get recording before we run out of studio time, plus I have other things to do today."

CHAPTER ELEVEN

JORDYN

I pick up enough of the conversation between Scott and Asher by reading Scott's lips to know what was being said between the two. I feel like I need to hide myself from Scott's view. I know Asher is only trying to help and be protective, but if this band thing is going to work he is going to have to let me fly on my own. The point of today's recording is to see if this is going to work. Starting it off with him having to speak with the manager on things that need to change for me probably isn't the best start.

I watch Scott as he tells Asher to basically relax. All I can see from Asher is the back of his head nodding. I can't see any part of his face to see what his reaction to Scott's words may be.

I have to admit, my heart sinks a little. I know what I'm feeling for Asher, and it's all probably happening way too quickly. He's the lead singer of a very popular band. To say he's good looking is putting it mildly, top that off with his charm, any woman would be drawn to him and lose their heart. I'm definitely no exception. I need to be careful, though. I can't allow this to change me, or to forget why I'm here.

When he finally turns back toward me, all he is saying are the songs we were planning on singing. He doesn't look upset or frustrated, but that still doesn't settle my nerves and awareness.

Walking back into the room, he smiles, "You ready?"

Nodding, I hope my smile doesn't reflect the uncertain feelings I'm having at the moment.

The session took a couple of hours. Coming in today, I assumed we would be singing a couple of the songs, nothing really recorded other than maybe to listen back to, but Scott had other plans. I'm thinking this is something to get used to. The man seems to be always thinking ten steps in front of anyone else. That may be why he is such a great manager and how this band hit it big as fast as they did once under his wings.

We ended up fully recording. Scott says once the ink is set on my contract, he is ready to release the new member of the band out onto the world. Which now brings us to the very large conference room we have all moved into and a couple contracts sitting in front of me on the table.

The whole band is still here, along with Steven. As I flip through the stack of papers in front of me, I'm wishing Mr. Emly was here as well. These things are never worded easily and I'm hoping I'm understanding enough of it.

A tap on my shoulder brings my attention to my right

where Steven is sitting. "If you have questions, Jordyn, please ask. Lawyer wording can be a bit intimidating."

Offering him a thankful smile, I continue on with reading through one of the largest, life-changing stacks of papers I've ever read.

Another hour pushes by and I believe I have a pretty good idea of what I'm signing onto. My pen lingers over the signature line and I take a moment to look around the table.

"Are you guys sure you are all agreeing with this? You've been doing great as the band that you are. Adding my signature to this line, from what I'm reading, means you are stuck with me for a little while."

Noah stands up from his chair and leans over the table, his finger tapping on the stack of papers in front of me. "Jordyn, sign the contract so that we can go get some food. Scott has kept us here long enough and has no intention of feeding us from what I'm guessing."

Looking over at Asher, he looks relaxed, sitting back in his chair, but I see the slight shake of his knee. Today's earlier conversation between him and Scott comes back and I'm wondering what he's thinking at this moment. Since everyone is here, I'm thinking this is the perfect moment to make something very clear to everyone.

"Before I sign, I do have something I want to say. This opportunity is something I only thought would stay as a dream for me. Sitting here, realizing the only thing standing in the way of that dream is my signature, is very surreal. You all have been amazing with making me feel like this is the perfect fit for me. I don't think most groups would be so laid back about bringing in a new member which tells me a lot about each of you. Bringing in a female is one thing, but a deaf female..."

Zayden's hands raise above his head and he starts waving them enthusiastically, stopping me and bringing my attention to him, "Wait...you're a girl?"

There it is. I don't need the words of warning and assurance I was going to give them about being around a deaf person and how I can take care of myself. I realize I need to take this day by day. The fame, the relationship, and I think I can confidently say, my new family. Something is telling me I'm going from one very protective brother to five more and Asher.

My hand seems to be moving in slow motion across the page, the ink scribbling out my name.

Steven flips through the pages and points out where signatures and initials are required. With each line signed my excitement takes over my nerves. The last line and it's official, I'm a member of Driven Roads.

I know my smile probably says it all, my cheeks hurt from how big it is. I have a whole family of people to text and let them know the news, but on the other side of it, I want to get into my Jeep and just drive, alone, and let everything soak in and take in everything that is about to happen, because something tells me after today, alone time isn't going to be often and I'm all right with that.

Jumping as my chair starts to slide back on me, I look over my shoulder to find Asher standing behind me. "How about some lunch?"

I'm starving, but I have so many people who are

waiting for me to give them the news about how today went.

Dean pops up next to Asher. "I'm going to pass out soon if I don't get some food. Why don't we all go to that burger joint down the street?"

Lunch with the band, not just Asher and myself. It probably wouldn't look good if I make excuses to not go right after signing on with them. From the irritated look Asher is throwing at Dean, I'm thinking Asher wasn't looking at a group date. I have to stop myself from smiling.

The stack of contracts slide away from in front of me by Scott. "I'd love to join you guys, however, now my work day is just beginning. I have promotional photoshoots to set up and music to get ready for release. We have a new member to introduce to your fans."

Dawson stands, "Looks like the tabloids have beaten you to it, Scott." He flips his phone around for us to see the screen.

There it is, a picture of Asher and me, kissing! Headline, "Is Asher James of Driven Roads off the market?"

The picture was taken this morning out in the parking lot. My excitement fades a little. The ink isn't even dry on the contracts yet and I've already hit the tabloids.

My phone vibrates in my pocket, but before I can reach for it Noah comes up next to me and wraps an arm around my shoulder. "Welcome to the band. It's out that my brother is off the market, now just wait to see what the headlines say once they find out you aren't just any girl, but the new member."

Asher pushes him away, "Really, man?"

Scott is already moving toward the door, but before he

leaves he turns to us. "This is why I need to get to work." He looks directly at me, "I'll be emailing you over a schedule by tonight, Jordyn."

I can't find any words at the moment. I just nod my acknowledgment and smile. Again my phone vibrates. Grabbing it from my back pocket, I have a couple texts from my brother.

Justin: Still thinking you don't need a bodyguard?

That text is followed by the image we just saw on Dawson's phone.

Asher squeezes my shoulder. I forgot he was standing behind me. "Who is that?"

"My brother, Justin."

"He thinks you need a bodyguard?"

"He is a bodyguard, that's his profession. Add that to being the overprotective brother."

"You can drive to the diner with me, just leave your Jeep here for the time being. That will give you a little time to text your family. Why don't you invite your brother to join us, maybe him meeting us will make him feel a little more relaxed."

There is nothing that is going to relax my brother. I have a feeling protective was understated. Now he is going to become impossible. Here I was worried about the band dealing with me and the adjustments. I think I may have been worried about the wrong people.

I quickly send a text to Justin asking if he would like to join us and his response is instant.

Justin: I will be there in fifteen minutes.

CHAPTER TWELVE

ASHER

The whole time Jordyn was reading through the contract, I found myself going over the brief conversation earlier with Scott. He was right. She doesn't need someone standing up for her and making sure the world is rotating perfectly for her. She is deaf, she is managing just fine. I think I'm the one that needs to make the adjustments. She isn't the type that likes to be coddled, normally we men look for that. Here I was coddling her, though. She is independent, smart and has adapted. She stands on her own two feet and that's what attracted me to her to begin with. I'm the one who needs to remember all of this.

It seems that someone already has the overprotective role covered anyway. I can't say that I blame the guy. From the story she told me about the accident, any older brother would be reacting the same way. That's why I suggested he come and meet us.

Jordyn handled the tabloid picture well. There are going to be lots of those and most of the headlines aren't always going to be truthful, but standing on this side of them, you almost need to learn to find the humor in them.

"Finally, time to eat." Noah follows Scott out the door.

Jordyn stands up, turns to me, and takes a deep breath. "So, how does it feel?"

"There isn't any one word to describe it. I'm excited, nervous, overwhelmed, and have had to stop from pinching myself a handful of times to make sure this isn't a dream."

"I've thought the same thing since meeting you. This must all be a dream."

Heavy hands clamp down on my shoulders and Jesse's voice comes from behind, "Man, that was very corny."

Jordyn's laughter fills the room, "It was a little corny."

"Now I have you teaming up with them. They don't need any encouragement."

"Sorry." She isn't trying real hard to hide her smile.

"No you're not," Zayden comments as he walks to the door and follows Noah out, the rest of the guys following behind him.

It's just Jordyn and me in the room now. "On a serious note, you all good with the picture?"

Her shoulders come up in a slight shrug. "It made all of this that much more real. Sign a contract, bam, you are in the tabloids, but it wasn't so bad. You have more to lose from it than I do, it says you are off the market."

Wrapping an arm around her waist, I bring her tight up to my chest. "The moment you tapped my chest and told me to feel the beat, I was off the market."

I want to make sure she has no doubt in her mind about what I'm feeling for her. "Jordyn, I'm not one of those guys who's afraid to voice my feelings. That first day in the studio, you started reeling me in with your voice. At dinner, when you asked everyone how they felt about you joining us, that tightened the line, then at my house yesterday, that hook sank so far in."

"You do realize you just described all of that in fishing terms." She is laughing at me.

"My country roots pop up every now and again."

Her smile falls, "Asher, I read Scott's lips earlier today in the studio. I couldn't tell what started the conversation, but I caught enough."

Damn, one thing to remember. She may miss some conversations, but she is going to pick up on some as well with the ability to read lips like she can.

"I was getting on them for not making sure you were aware they were talking. Scott was setting me straight on being overprotective. I'm going to mess up, Jordyn. I get what your brother is feeling when it comes to being protective over you. You are completely capable of handling yourself. Scott was reminding me of that."

Closing the space between us, she kisses me. It was sweet and fast. "Thank you for looking out for me, but Scott is right, Asher. I'm going to miss some things, I'm going to look lost every once in a while. All in all, it's usually nothing that important, but if it is something important, I know you will be there to fill me in."

Yes, definitely hooked. "You know this means you are off the market as well."

"No one cares if I'm off the market, no one knows who I am."

"If Scott is on it, everyone is going to know exactly who you are by tonight. You ready for this?"

"I hope so. I just signed a bunch of papers saying I'm stuck."

The door opens again to the room, and Noah's head pops in. "Look, we are starving out here, are you two done so we can go get some food?"

"No one said you had to wait for us," I reminded him.

Jordyn takes a step back and I have no choice but to release her. She grabs her bag off the floor by her chair, takes my hand, and leads the way to the door. "My brother will be waiting. We should be going."

The ride was short to the diner, and Jordyn spent it typing away on her phone. Pulling into the driveway, my eyes instantly find a truck with a large man leaned up against the back of it.

Tapping Jordyn's leg, her eyes come up from her phone and look over at me. "I'm going to assume that is your brother?" I point out the front windshield.

Jordyn's eyes follow where I'm pointing and her head begins to bob up and down. "Yep, that would be Justin. I'm just going to apologize now."

Jordyn is opening the door and jumping down from the passenger seat before I even shift the truck into park.

Jumping down myself, I meet the rest of the guys, who are all standing in the parking lot not far from Jordyn and her brother, just watching. It's quite the sight. Jordyn is maybe as tall as her brother's chest, and her hands are moving fast in front of her.

"I'm wishing I knew sign language just to know what she is saying to him. That is one large man and she is controlling that conversation." Noah has a look of amusement on his face.

Walking over, I go and stand next to Jordyn, stretching my hand out to Justin. "Hi, I'm Asher."

"Justin." He shakes my hand and the extra strength in the shake doesn't go unnoticed.

Nor does the glare of warning shooting out of Jordyn's eyes toward her brother. Not going to lie. The guy is a little intimidating. I wouldn't consider myself a short guy at six feet tall, but this guy towers over me. Between his height and the build on him, it's no wonder he is in the profession he is.

CHAPTER THIRTEEN

JORDYN

My glare toward my brother is met with one right back at me. He isn't going to go easy with Asher, and I didn't expect him to, I just don't want him to be rude.

"These guys behind me are the rest of the band. Noah, Jesse, Dean, Zayden, and Dawson." Asher makes a quick introduction of the guys.

Each in turn come over and shake my brother's hand. All in all it's kind of comical to watch. Neither of the guys look to be intimidated by my brother, but each have a respectful look in their eyes for the size of him. He gets that look everywhere we go.

"All right, man, I need to ask, how damn tall are you?" Noah pipes up after each have greeted him.

The smile my brother gives has me relaxing a little.

"I missed seven feet by a few inches," Justin answers, standing tall and proud of his height.

"So what you are saying is there isn't a door you can go

into without ducking." Noah continues with the questions.

"Noah, really?" Asher pipes in before my brother answers.

"What? He can't take offense to the questions. The guy must get them everywhere he goes." Noah stands next to Justin and stretches up onto his toes, trying to reach my brother's height.

Not even close.

Justin looks down at Noah next to him with a look of "you wish, man."

"Come on, guys. If you are done now with comparing sizes, I'm hungry." I start the walk toward the diner, not even looking back to see if they are following.

Once we sit down, the questions start to fly out of my brother's mouth.

"When do you guys go back on tour?"

Asher pulls out his phone and starts tapping around on the screen. "We leave for Arizona next Wednesday."

"So you guys are performing at Country Stampede?" Justin asks.

"Yes."

"I'm already scheduled to be there." Justin smiles.

It doesn't go unnoticed how relieved he looks that the schedule seemed to work with his. He is going to have to get over the fact that he isn't going to be with me everywhere we go.

"I'm at that event every year. What does your security look like?" Justin ask.

"Really, Justin, do we need to talk about all of this now?" I sign to him.

"Yes," he uses his voice with his hands. "You hit the tabloids before the ink was probably dry on the contracts today."

"Unfortunately, that probably was more because of me than anything," Asher pipes in. "Justin, I understand the whole being protective thing, I don't blame you. You are her brother and I want you to hear it from me. I'm not hiding my relationship with Jordyn from the world, so there will probably be lots more images like the one that went out today, the paparazzi live for that stuff. Once it gets announced that she is now a member of Driven Roads, that information is just going to feed them more. We have two guys that travel with us everywhere we go when we are out on the road and then of course we have extra security everywhere we perform."

Justin sits in silence. His silence is louder than his words sometimes. He is gauging Asher, but I'm sure no one else is noticing the little more respect he has for Asher that I see in his eyes right now.

My heart fluttered a little faster when Asher said he wasn't going to hide our relationship from everyone. Trying to remind oneself to not fall too fast is a little harder when someone says stuff like that. It's not the first time he has said it today either.

"I know the music world well," Justin finally speaks up. "Jordyn, on the other hand, doesn't..."

"Stop," I hold up my hand to stop my brother. "I'm not a child, Justin. Yes, you are right. I haven't been around the scene much, but I'm not ignorant either. Believe it or not I can take care of myself."

Justin turns an angry glare toward me. "No one said you were ignorant, Jordyn, but let's bring up the obvious. You are deaf."

"Yes, which I have been dealing with most of my life. Justin, I love you, but you are going to have to let me fall every once in a while. I'm going to be all right."

"I'll make sure she doesn't fall." Asher has direct eye contact with Justin.

"You guys do realize that at some point, I will be alone."

Every guy sitting around the table is looking at me shaking their head no. I was right when earlier I figured I've gone from one overprotective brother to five more and a boyfriend. Oh my gosh, boyfriend. That is the first time I have, even to myself, referred to Asher as my boyfriend. I'm thinking the first person I'm going to be texting after this lunch is Megan. If I'm going to be traveling with this group, I'm going to be bringing backup with me.

The rest of lunch is the guys talking and me just watching. I'm pretty sure the guys passed my brother's inspection process and it's a really good sign that he and Asher are talking about more than just protection detail for me.

Asher ends up paying for everyone's lunch. Not sure if he is trying to impress my brother or just felt like he would treat everyone.

After saying goodbye for another thirty minutes in the parking lot, Asher takes me back to my Jeep.

"Would you be opposed to coming back to my place?" Asher asks before I can get out of the truck.

It's a very tempting offer, but it has been a very eventful day. I still have my parents who are waiting on me to let them know more about what is going on and I'm sure Megan is going crazy waiting for me to get home.

"I really want to say yes, but there is so much for me to do and people waiting to talk to me. I haven't had a chance to really tell them much except I signed the contracts. I haven't even spoken to Mr. Emly yet. I think it's best if I stop by my parents' for a little while and then head home for the evening."

The disappointment in Asher's eyes is very obvious and it takes a lot of self-control on my part to not give in and say yes, but I need a little time today. A lot has happened and I have a feeling it's going to get a little crazy.

"I would like to convince you to change your mind, but I understand. Will you have dinner with me tomorrow night?"

"Are you asking me out on a date, Mr. James?"

"The first of many." Leaning over to me, his hand goes around my neck and pulls me in to meet his lips.

"You know you aren't making it very easy for me to get out of this truck."

"Good, that was my plan."

Temptation is a dangerous thing, I want nothing more than to follow this man home, but I have a lot of people waiting to hear from me and something tells me that I'm going to be very busy starting tomorrow.

"Text me tomorrow with what time to be ready." I kiss

him quickly one last time and hurry to open the door and let myself out of the truck, getting into my own vehicle before I change my mind.

Once my door closes, I look up and see Asher watching me still from the driver's seat of his truck. I want to pinch myself. This is my life now. I just signed on with Driven Roads, I have a boyfriend and if I'm not mistaken, I believe he told my brother he wasn't going anywhere.

Turning my key in the ignition, I wave one last time at Asher, and pull out of the parking spot. Each moment I sit here is one more moment I have to change my mind and go with him back to his place.

One thing hasn't gone unnoticed. I texted Mr. Emly earlier today and when I glanced quickly at my phone before leaving the studio, I hadn't received a text message back from him. This isn't like him. I want to share the news with him, although I'm pretty sure everyone knew I was going to sign, I mean who wouldn't? All in all, though, it's still news I want to share with him and thank him again for making this happen. Once I get to my parents' house I'll have to try and text him again.

It's no real surprise that when I pull up to my parents' house, I find my brother's truck in the driveway. I should have guessed it wouldn't have been as easy as lunch and a hug goodbye.

Checking my phone one more time before I go inside and get bombarded with the million questions, there is still no answer from Mr. Emly, but I do have a few new messages from Megan.

I send her a quick text back.

Me: Just pulled up at my parents, I'll text when I'm leaving and we can get together.

Megan: Girl, this waiting thing is killing me. I need details.

She isn't referring to the details of me signing contracts, she is wanting the details about Asher.

Me: I promise to let you know the minute I'm leaving.

Megan: Fine, talk to you soon.

Movement up at the house catches my eye and there stands Amber with Kylie and my mom. Into the firing squad I go.

Making my way to the front door where they are waiting for me, my niece is the first thing I give my attention to. "How is my girl?"

I reach out for her and Amber lets me take her into my arms, but that only frees up her hands to start firing off the questions. "So, Asher James, I need details," she signs.

"No questions about signing with the largest country band, or anything like that?" I ask, knowing they are excited but want more details about Asher.

"We have plenty of time to talk about the group, we want to know about the hot man who seems, by what your brother has told us, very taken by you." My mom's hands are the next to start asking the questions.

"Can we at least go inside first?"

"Your dad and brother are playing their parts in you having a new, not to mention famous boyfriend. We want the good information before you have to hold back because they are around," Amber explains.

"There isn't much to tell, yet. Yes, Asher and I have a

connection." I give little detail and see both my mom and sister-in-law roll their eyes.

"Details," Amber signs.

I have been very fortunate. Growing up, my mother and I have always been close. I could talk to her about anything. She always said she would rather keep a clear line of communication between herself and her children than have them hiding things from her. She would keep an open mind, we wouldn't hide things from them. So having this conversation with her isn't weird at all.

"There isn't much to say as of yet. Yes, we have kissed. Yes, it was amazing. Tomorrow night we are going out on our first date, I guess you can say. More details to follow soon."

"Don't tell your brother that I've told you this, he is trying to keep up the persona of tough bigger brother, but he admitted that Asher isn't a bad guy. For your brother, that's big."

My brother's size fools only those who don't know him. He is actually a gentle giant.

"Come on, we better get inside, before your father comes looking for us. His chest is so pumped out with pride. It's kind of cute," my mom signs, then turns to lead the way into the house.

CHAPTER FOURTEEN

ASHER

The house is quiet and I'm marveling over how differently I look at silence now. Walking out the back door, I hear the quiet hum of the pool filter, the gentle sound of the air under a bird's wings as it flies down over my head and settles on a limb of the tree next to me. The leaves on the trees as they rustle in the slight breeze. All the sounds we don't really listen to, the common sounds of the day that most people take for granted. Sitting down in one of the chairs, I let my head fall back against the back and close my eyes.

In the distance I can hear cars pass on the street. A dog barking somewhere, all of the sounds that fill the world around us. Jordyn hears none of this. She started life with sound, but losing it at such a young age, a child doesn't think about taking time to hear the sounds around them, just in case something was to happen to take it away. I wonder if she remembers them, or like many memories, they have faded as she has gotten older.

Yesterday is still lingering in my mind. I still feel her arms around me as she showed me to feel the strum of the guitar. I remember feeling the hitch in the breath she took and that's when I knew she was feeling the same as I was. That's when I knew I had to kiss her. That kiss, though, that was it. The moment I tasted those lips I knew I'd do anything for her and anything to make her mine.

The doorbell sounds throughout the house. I'm not expecting anyone. The slight hope that it may be Jordyn is the only thing that gets me motivated enough to get out of my chair and go see who has decided to stop by. Usually my brother or the guys will text that they are on their way. Not asking, just informing, so I'm not thinking it's one of them.

Looking through the large frosted glass section of the front door, I see a male figure standing there.

Opening the door, I see the last person I ever thought would be standing there. "Sean?"

"Hey, Asher, I hope you don't mind me stopping by. I wanted to talk with you, that is if you have a few minutes."

He looks different, almost tired. I move to the side, "Absolutely, come on in."

He steps in and waits for me to lead the way. "I hope you don't mind that Scott gave me your address."

"No, I don't mind at all. Is everything all right?" I lead us into the large living room and point to the couch, inviting him to take a seat. "Would you like something to drink?"

Shaking his head no, he takes a seat on the couch, I follow and sit in the chair facing the couch. "How did everything go today?"

I'm a little confused as to why he is here if only to find out how the day went. I would have thought Jordyn had already told her mentor that she signed on with the group.

"It went well. Jordyn, I'm guessing you know already, signed on with the group. The group went out for a celebration lunch, where we met Justin."

Sean laughs, but it doesn't go unnoticed how weak it sounds. "Justin is a great guy. However, he is very protective of his sister. I wouldn't be surprised if he quits his other job to become her full-time bodyguard now that she has signed."

"Funny you say that. At lunch he seemed very relieved that he is already hired on by Country Stampede to be there."

"How did he take the image flying across the Internet?"

So that's why Sean stopped by. "Sean, I'm not going to hide the relationship I'm hoping to build with Jordyn. I'm sure that isn't going to be the last picture to fly across social media news."

He doesn't say anything, but sits there nodding his head. I feel like I'm sitting across from a father who is trying to gauge out his daughter's new boyfriend.

"You think it's wise to introduce her into the music world this way?"

"No disrespect, Sean, I understand the concern, but I also think sometimes the men in her life, meaning you and Justin, I haven't met her father yet, are forgetting she isn't some fragile little girl. Actually quite the opposite, which is one of the many things that has attracted me to her. Her determination to not allow that fact that she can't hear stop her from doing what she loves in a world where hearing is a key factor just proves her strength. She showed me a very small example of what she feels in the music and I'm amazed at what I've been missing out with something I love and is a huge part of my life. I personally think that the hearing world may be missing out a little. What you have taught Jordyn to feel and understand about music is amazing and I can't wait to learn more and to see where things will go between the two of us. So if you stopped by hoping to convince me to step away from the feelings I have developing for Jordyn, then I'm sorry, but that's not happening."

The slight smile that Sean seems very hard trying to suppress doesn't go unnoticed. "The first time that little girl opened her mouth and I heard her sing my heart tore apart for a little girl who's only dream was to be a singers but heard no sound. Her eyes looked so sad when I met her, but the way they lite up when she was singing proved to me she would be willing to work hard to have a slight chance to fulfilling a dream that one person's wrong decision threaten to take away from her. It's hard not to feel protective over her, but trust me when I say, and I speak for Justin as well I'm sure, her determination to overcome those obstacles that were placed in her path proves that she is very capable of handling this and shows the strength she has to handle just about anything. I'll be honest Asher, my coming by here today wasn't over the concern of what was going to be thrown at her by the world, but to make sure what's being thrown at her heart."

So that's what this is all about. Sean is worried that I'm going to hurt Jordyn. "Sean, no one knows what will happen tomorrow or ten years down the road. I can't sit here and tell you that a relationship between Jordyn and I, is going to be perfect, nothing is perfect. However, what I can tell you is that my plans aren't to have a little fun and then push her aside. My plan is to learn from her this amazing skill that you have taught her, and to continuing falling hard for a woman who has taken my world and flipped it upside down."

Studying me for a moment, finally the smile that he has been trying very hard to suppress splits across his lips. Nodding his head as though he is telling himself he is convinced by my response, he stands up from the couch and starts to walk back toward the front door. I stand, following him.

Opening the door, he turns to me once again. "Take care of her and give her the world that she deserves."

His tired eyes, slow speech, the way his shoulders are slightly rounded forward and now his words, I'm worried. "Sean, is there something else going on?"

I'm not sure how else to ask if he is all right, but from the way he tries to stand a little taller with my question, I think he understands what I'm trying to ask.

"I'm good. I just wanted to make sure Jordyn is and will continue to be treated right."

I still think there is more than what he is telling me, but I don't know the man well enough to feel that's it's my place to keep pushing the issue. Nodding my understanding, I watch as he walks down the porch steps and back to his car.

Shutting the front door, I pull out my phone and pull up Jordyn's number.

Me: Are you home yet?

Her response comes back only seconds later.

Jordyn: Just walked in the door.

Me: Are you sure you don't want to come over?

Jordyn: Megan is on her way over. If I push her off one more time, I may just lose my best friend.

Me: Fine! What time can I pick you up tomorrow?

Jordyn: I have no plans tomorrow, so whenever you would like.

Me: I'll be there at 10:00, need your address please.

Jordyn: I thought we were going to dinner?

Me: Not enough time, I'm thinking the whole day if you are up to it.

Jordyn: I'll be ready at 10:00. See you in the morning.

Another text follows after with her address and I find myself smiling as I head back to my music room. Inspiration for a song has me wanting to write down some lyrics before I forget them.

CHAPTER FIFTEEN

JORDYN

Setting my bag down in the chair at the dining room table, my phone vibrates in my pocket. It's Asher. At the same time, my front door flies open and Megan lets herself in.

"You just walked in the door and he is already texting you?" She comes around my back and reads the text message over my shoulder as Asher and I chat.

I feel her head shake back and forth and then nod against my shoulder. Looking over my shoulder, I ask, "Are you talking to yourself?"

"I guess so, you can't hear me! Who would have thought, my best friend would be the one who wraps Asher James around her finger."

"I'm guessing you saw the picture that posted today?"

Megan rolls her eyes and plops down onto the couch. "Who hasn't seen the picture of you two making out in the parking lot?"

"We weren't making out."

"Yeah, right! I don't blame you, my friend. You're that

girl that every female in the United States wants to be right now. So, tell me about today."

"I signed the contracts and am an official member of Driven Roads. Justin called and freaked out about the photo, so we met him for lunch with the band. Went to my parents and now I'm here."

"Wait, Justin met you guys for lunch? Did he flip out?"

"No, he tried the whole, 'I'm the older protective brother' thing," I throw my fingers up in air quotes, "but all in all it wasn't bad. I think he liked that Asher wasn't intimidated by him. Plus, he likes that next week when we are at Country Stampede, he'll be there as well."

"You guys are performing at Country Stampede? Jordyn, that's huge."

"Actually that is something I want to talk to you about. How would you like to come with us? Kind of like my assistant, actually, it's a little more than that."

"What do you mean more?"

I can see the excitement radiating through my friend as she is trying to control it. She has moved to the edge of the couch and it's taking every ounce of will power to not jump up and scream out her answer.

"While I was at my parents' house the subject came up about an interpreter, I reached out to Scott and we've been texting back and forth quite a bit and he is agreeing with everything. I'd feel a lot better having an assistant/interrupter with me when we are out and touring. I know you have a job now as an assistant that you love, but what would say about working full-time with me?"

"Let me make sure I'm understanding everything. You

want me to quit my job and become your personal assistant/interrupter? I would travel with you and the band everywhere? Doing the same thing basically I'm doing now, but for my best friend and touring with a bunch of hot men?"

Nodding, I confirm everything she is asking. Before I know it she is up off the couch and in my arms hugging me.

"I'm hoping this is a yes. I know I'm asking a lot, especially the whole quitting the job you have now, but I can't think of anyone else I would want to be there with me."

Megan takes a step back, "I don't even have to think about it," her hands start moving in front of me, "there is nothing my job could offer for me to stay. I'll put my two-week notice in tomorrow. If they need me when we have to leave for Country Stampede, I'll work remote for a week or so."

Wrapping my arms around my best friend, I pull her in for another hug, excited that this new journey is going to be a little easier with her by my side.

Pulling out of my arms, Megan goes right into work mode. "I'll need to get ahold of Scott and get the schedule, introduce myself and make sure we have all communication linked."

Holding up my hands, I stop Megan's pacing and chatting. She isn't really talking to me so I'm only catching half of what she is saying. "Megan, stop. Scott is sending me a schedule tomorrow and I'll make sure I set up a meeting between the two of you as soon as possible. For tonight, I think we need to order some pizza, watch a couple of movies and relax. Something tells me after tonight, there won't be much time for just the two of us to hang out. Plus, you don't even know the pay yet, you may change your mind."

"I won't lie, I'd probably be all right with working for free, that is if I didn't have bills I needed to pay, but you are right. Tonight, we relax and eat pizza, but instead of the movie, you get to tell me what it's like to be with Asher James."

It's nine-twenty and I'm ready for when Asher comes to pick me up. I haven't slept much and have to admit that I've been ready since about seven this morning. Megan ended up leaving around one and I haven't slept much since then. I feel like a high school girl waiting on her first date with the boy she's had a crush on all year.

The reality on yesterday's events hit hard about three o'clock this morning. It was like my excited high hit a low and complete realization hit of what signing those contracts actually meant. I signed contracts binding me to Driven Roads. I'm going to be on stage in front of thousands of people and to top it off, I'm kicking off with Country Stampede, the largest country music festival in the United States. It's a full weekend of the best country music out there today and I'm going to be on stage with one of the largest bands performing. To top everything off, I opened up social media to find the picture of Asher and I in the parking lot of the studio kissing still plastered everywhere. My face is already everywhere and I haven't even been announced as a new member of the group yet. Right now I'm Asher James' new girl.

The lights in the apartment begin to flash letting me know someone is at my front door. Looking at the clock, it's only nine-thirty, he's early.

Opening the door I find Asher in jeans and a black button-up shirt, cowboy hat in hand. "Sorry, I'm a little early, I couldn't wait in the parking lot any longer."

His arm loops around my waist and he pulls me tight up against him, his lips instantly finding mine. My arms come up and around his shoulders, my fingers digging into the hair at the back of his head. His chest vibrates against mine, a feeling I'm finding ignites a need in me. I can't hear his responses to my touches and kisses, but I can feel them throughout my entire body.

He fists the back of my shirt in his hand, a sign I'm reading as his need for me may be just as deep as mine is for him.

Something brushes down my leg before it settles on the floor at my feet. His other hand comes up and tangles itself into my long hair, up to my nape and he holds my head tight to his as his tongue searches out mine.

I feel the temperature change of his body and the hardened proof of his need for me, and again, the vibration from his chest to mine that pulses through to my core. My need to be free of anything between us is becoming hard to ignore and just when I think I can't take anymore and find myself begging for him, he ends the kiss.

We stand in front of my open apartment door, for anyone who may walk by to see, forehead to forehead, our breathing rapid. He still has a tight hold on me, like if he lets go I'm going to disappear, and I realize I don't care who may pass by and what they may see, I have no desire to move from his hold.

Our breathing begins to even out and the hold he has releases. He takes a small step back and I find I have to catch my balance without his arms around me. I watch as he bends down and picks his hat up off the floor. I take the few quick moments to inhale deeply and try to cool the fire still scorching throughout my entire body.

Placing his hat on his head, I take in the sight before me. I watch his arm muscles flex under his shirt and as my eyes travel up, against the black of his hat, his blue eyes are shining like a blue flame of a very hot fire.

"Good morning." His small smile does something to me and I have to fight my need to throw myself back into his arms.

Shoving my hands into my back pockets to keep them from reaching out to him, I smile back. "Good morning."

"Ready?"

If he only knew how ready! Nodding, I turn and grab my bag and follow him out of the door, locking it behind me.

Opening the passenger door for me, he stops me before I can climb up into the seat. His hand gently cups the side of my face and his lips find mine for the second time this morning. This time, though, his lips are soft against mine and the kiss is light, but it takes my breath away just the same.

The kiss is over as quickly as it started. "I want you all to myself today before I have to share you with the world. So, I have planned a little drive and a location that we won't have to worry about photographers and what ends up on the news tomorrow."

"Yes, it's amazing how far they can stretch one image."

"And because they only have that one image, it's going to cause a frenzy and they are going to be everywhere trying to get the next best shot."

"So you are saying no more privacy?"

"The moment the ink hit the contract you gave up privacy. Once they find out the mystery woman in the photo is the new member of the group, it's going to be a feeding frenzy for the piranhas of social media."

CHAPTER SIXTEEN

ASHER

Leaning forward, I kiss her one more time and stand back so that she can climb up into the passenger seat. Before I shut the door I touch her leg, bringing her attention back to me from buckling her seatbelt. "If I was a true country gentleman, I'd stand back and allow you time to adjust to the fame before we add the relationship, but Jordyn, as proof was presented this morning, I can't stay away from you and I have no plans on trying."

She leans forward as far as the seatbelt will allow and closes the space between us with her hand at the back of my neck, pulling me up to meet her lips. It's a quick kiss but I feel the heat and need behind it.

"We've got this." She smiles and I'm relieved that she is feeling the same way I do.

Shutting the door, I quickly round the front of the truck and jump into the driver's seat.

Starting up the engine, my music blares throughout

the cab. I reach to turn it down, but her hand reaches out to stop me. "No, leave it."

I'm sure the puzzlement on my face speaks my unasked question for me. Jordyn laughs, "I feel the vibration through my seat. It must be pretty loud."

"I admit, I drive with it loud." I feel like I'm screaming at her and realize there isn't a need to try and compete with the volume of the radio as long as she can see my lips.

She reaches for my hand, "Find me the beat."

Placing my hand on the center console of my truck, her hand now on top of mine, I quickly find the beat of the song, my hand now tapping along with it.

"Sing it for me, please."

It happens to be one of my favorites and I start to sing along. I feel her eyes on me as she watches every word. Before I know it, she is singing along in perfect pitch and in precise timing.

After the song, I turn the radio down. Not only did I feel like a fool because I found myself trying to yell over it, but I couldn't hear her either.

"Do you have the words to every song memorized?"

She laughs and shakes her head no. "That is one of my favorites. I read through the words of songs when they release. If the words tug at me, I learn them. I'll tell you a secret, though. In my car, the radio screen announces the song playing. I'm sure for anyone driving next to me my car is vibrating because I have it turned up extremely loud to feel the vibration of the beat, and I sing along probably just as loud, but I'm sure completely off tempo."

She really has no idea how her voice grabs a person

and draws them in. "Jordyn, even off tempo people would stop to listen to your voice, trust me."

Rolling her eyes, she gives me the "whatever" look.

After driving for about an hour and a half, I turn off the main road onto a dirt road. I've been to this place so many times, I could probably drive it blind folded, but the road has been washed out a little and it tosses the truck around a bit. On both sides of the road are large meadows. The road may be a little rutted but the view is amazing.

Thirty minutes pass and the lake comes into view.

"Asher, it is beautiful. I've lived around here my entire life and I didn't know this place was here."

After being nervous this morning wondering if this would be a place she would enjoy going to, I'm relieved that she is excited.

Parking the truck under a large tree with lots of shade, Jordyn, is jumping out of the passenger seat before I can get to her side to open the door.

Like every other time I've been here, there isn't another person around. I figured this would be the perfect place to have a little time with Jordyn without worrying who is watching and waiting to take the next best picture of us.

Opening the backseat door, I start to grab stuff that I brought.

"What can I help with?" When I turn she is standing directly behind me.

Handing her the blanket and guitar, I grab everything

else and walk to the other side of the large tree I parked under and start setting everything down and arranging it.

"I brought food for lunch, are you hungry?"

No response. Turning, I find her kicking her boots off then she kneels down onto the blanket I just spread out, "What can I help with?"

I did it again. It's hard not to react even if just with a facial expression because she watches everything so closely that someone does so that she doesn't miss something. If I react she is going to know I once again messed up and forgot I can't speak to her when she is behind me.

"Nothing really," I try to act as normal as I can, "there is this great sub shop down in town, so I grabbed a couple of sandwiches and some mixed fresh fruit they had. I wasn't sure what you would like."

"I'm not picky, I eat just about anything."

I'm pretty sure I got away with my slip up, or she is just being nice and ignoring it to make me feel better. Whichever it may be, I'm glad we are moving past it.

Together we spread the food out. Settled with my back against the tree and sandwich in hand, I realize how much I've missed coming up here.

"How did you know about this place?"

"My father would bring my brother and me up here and we would camp and fish. I haven't been here for a few years, I just thought this would be a good place to spend a quiet day."

"It's a great place."

I watch as she looks around, the way her expressions change, she'll smile, then squint, a few times she has closed her eyes.

Leaning over I tap her hand, getting her attention. "You were ten when you lost your hearing, do you remember any of the sounds?"

Shrugging, she replies, "I'd like to think I do, yes. At ten, though, what child pays that much attention to the sounds of the world around them? Some say I'm one of the lucky ones, I had years of hearing before the silence. There are times where I believe it would have been better to not know what I was missing."

"What sound do you miss the most?"

She laughs, "You wouldn't believe me."

"Try me."

"It's the annoying sounds. The doorbell, alarm clocks, smoke detectors. Now everything flashes. Lights flash with the doorbell and smoke detectors. My bed shakes when the alarm goes off. I guess they are still considered annoying, not matter if it's the continuous beeping, or the continuous flashing and shaking."

That completely explains the sign on her front door that was posted saying to ring the doorbell. I'd thought to myself how odd that sounded, but now it makes complete perfect sense. How would she have heard a knock at the door?

"Although I have to admit, besides the sounds of music, which of course would be an obvious for me, I miss the sound of thunder. I love thunderstorms. My mom would come in and find my window wide open during storms so that I could listen to the thunder, hear the rain hitting the ground. Maybe it was because it sounded a little like music is why I loved it so much, but now like music, I feel the vibration of the thunder if it's large enough. The sound of it, though, I miss."

"If there was a sound you were given a chance to hear just once, what would it be?"

Her cheeks redden and her eyes leave mine as she looks around again. Sitting up from my leaned back position on the tree, I scoot closer to her. A finger under her chin, I bring her eyes back to mine.

"Never be embarrassed around me, Jordyn."

"You."

"What?"

She places her hand against my chest, "Your moans when you kiss me, I feel them against my chest and wish every time I feel that I could hear them. Your voice when you sing. I wish for just one minute I could hear you."

"If my heart didn't already completely belong to you, those words would have sealed it for me."

Her eyes go round with shock and I can almost see her mind trying to work through the words that she thinks I might have said, but is convinced there is no way she read my lips right.

"You read them right, Jordyn," I assure her. My hand goes from her chin to the back of her head and I bring her lips to mine.

At first the kiss is one-sided, but then it's like my words finally sink in and her lips start kissing me back. Relief washes over me. I basically just told her I was in love with her after only knowing each other a few days, but I know what I'm feeling for this woman and I'm not denying it.

CHAPTER SEVENTEEN

JORDYN

His words take me completely by surprise. He didn't actually say the words "I love you," but if I read them right, it was pretty close. It's been five days, can someone fall in love in five days? Absolutely, because if I'm being completely honest with myself, I'm falling in love with him.

His lips are demanding and the distance between us seems miles apart. Scooting up onto my knees, I make my way to his lap, straddling him.

There it is again, his chest vibrates and it ignites a need that I no longer want to push to the side, or worry it may be too soon. Asher has claimed my heart and right now, in this beautiful location, outside with mother nature surrounding us, I think is the perfect place and time to no longer hold back any of our feelings or needs. Taking advantage of the position I'm now in and the control I have, I press myself down onto him, letting him know what I want, and what I want right now is him, all of him, extinguishing the flames that he has ignited.

I can feel his skin warming up against my hands even through his shirt and I want the barrier of clothing between us gone, however, I don't want to rush it either. Pulling away just enough to get my hands in between us, but not breaking away from his kisses, I make work of the buttons on his shirt.

Working it down his shoulders, he helps remove it from his arms. My hands glide over his shoulders, and down his arms, tracing every muscle that I feel when he has them wrapped around me, knowing the strength he has and feeling the security within them.

My shirt is up and over my head, laying somewhere with his on the ground now. The only garment left as a barrier between the two of us being skin to skin follows quickly. Asher wraps his arms tightly around me and that first feel of his naked chest against mine is electrifying. I feel like I'm in a cocoon of safety and warmth wrapped up in his arms, but at the same time being struck by bolts of lightning.

My heads falls back, breaking our kiss and his lips find a place on my neck, where he lightly begins brushing kisses from my neck, across my shoulder and just the top of one breast. My hands go behind me, resting on his legs, leaning me back just enough to invite him to take more, I need him to take more!

This position also allows me to drive my hips into his, where I feel his hardness tight against his jeans. His lips are teasing me, as they lightly kiss around each of my breasts, taking careful strides not to touch the very tight and hardened nipple begging for his touch. My hands fist into the pant leg of his jeans to keep from grabbing his head and leading him to that spot.

One of his hands is at my back supporting me, the other is following his lips and brushing over each section of skin as his lips leave. I arch my back slightly, begging him to take what I'm offering. His tongue circles one tight nipple. Bringing my head up, our eyes meet as finally his lips suck in one tight bud, rolling his tongue around and sending a wave of shock through my body. I want to wrap myself around him tightly, inviting him to suck harder, but I don't want to lose the eye contact. Watching him as his tongue makes its way around and around the nipple, his eyes have almost turned to a white-blue. He actions have me grabbing the back of his head, pressing him tight to me, my hips driving into his.

"Asher," his name falls from my lips.

This brings his head back up and away from the amazing sensation he was creating. "Hold on, I've got you."

In one quick movement, he has me now lying on my back. He stands, and I watch as he quickly steps out of his boots, working with his belt and buttons on his jeans as he goes. Before I can plead for him to come back to me, he is standing there naked and I'm only able to stare. He bends down over me, his lips taking one breast into his mouth and then the other, then begin their journey down over my stomach.

I bring myself up onto my arms, needing to watch every inch his lips touch. Asher's lips trail back up, between the valley between my breasts and up to my neck.

My head falls back and I feel his hands making work of the belt and buttons of my jeans. His knuckles brush over the skin right under the zipper as he glides it down.

I lift my hips as he glides my jeans and any remaining garments down over them, making it easier for him. I had already taken off my boots, making the rest of undressing me easy. His eyes glide up my body and I watch as the need brightens in his eyes. My body is aching to have him touching me again, but at the same time, I don't want to stop watching the transformation of his desire through his eyes as they look at me.

His lips start at one of my shins, his hand following behind, directing my leg to bend as he trails his lips up over my knee, my thigh, and that's when I realize where is attention is heading. With my leg bent, it opens me up for him. His lips brush lightly over my heated center and I about come off the ground. My arms are shaking from holding me up, but I refuse to lie back and miss a moment of the desire and need in his eyes.

His tongue makes a slow swipe, and I feel the vibration of his moan from his chest against my leg and I about come apart. I bring one hand to his head and hold him to me, pleading with him for more. I see a slight smile spread across his lips before his tongue dips deep into my heated core and I know I must yell his name out, as my fingers dig into this hair and probably his scalp. My one arm holding me up gives in and I fall back, now arching my back to press myself into him.

His tongue is creating a sensation I've never felt before and the way my body is shaking on the inside, I know I'm close to losing myself. As much as I'm loving what his tongue is doing, I want him filling me when this release happens.

Both hands on his head, the hardest thing I've ever done is pull him away from me and lose that sensation, even just for a moment, of what he was starting to stir. His lips crash against mine, my hand glides down his sides and finds what I'm searching for. His hardness is heavy in my hand, wrapping my hand around him I begin to stroke him. His teeth bite down onto my lip and I arch into him.

I want nothing more than to please him as he did me, but he is holding me to him and now his hand is stopping mine from guiding him to me.

His lips leave mine and I open my eyes to look at him. "Wait," he tries to pull away from me and move my hand from him, "I need to get..."

I cut him off before he can move too far, my hand going back to guide him, "Asher, I'm on the pill. I don't want anything between us, I trust you."

"Jordyn," my name forms on his lips as he enters me.

I feel every inch of him as he fills me and I pull his lips down to mine to keep from screaming out. He moves one of his hands down my leg and once at my knee he begins to pull my leg up, wrapping his arm under my knee and opening my legs more as he pushes himself deeper. I'm at his mercy now. He pulls out and then drives back into me again. My eyes fly open and meet his only inches away.

"Don't close your eyes, Jordyn. Let me watch as you fall apart around me."

Those words are almost my undoing, but I need more of him. "More, Asher," I find myself begging.

I feel him pull back once again and thrust deeper this

time. It's slow and I can see the strength it's taking on his part not to move faster through the clutching of his jaw. I don't want him to hold back any more.

Pushing my leg out of his grasp, I wrap both of my legs around his waist, holding him tight inside of me and start to move with him. His movements quicken and it isn't long before I feel my release pulsing throughout my entire body.

I lock my ankles behind his back and hold on tight. He thrusts into me one last time and I watch his eyes cloud over as his gives into his release. My body rocks and pulls him in deeper and deeper with each pulse.

I have relaxed my legs from around him, but we don't move. I can feel his breathing as it evens out against my chest. We are forehead to forehead, our eyes locked. I'm afraid to blink, that everything might disappear.

If I had any questions about my feeling for Asher, they were clarified. I know how corny it is to say I know I'm in love with him, especially after having sex, but that wasn't just sex. Corny or not, I have fallen completely in love with Asher James.

He moves just to my right side, taking his weight off of his arms that are holding him up, and I instantly feel the cool breeze of the day hit the heated, now exposed skin. It feels amazing, but a part of me wants to grab him and bring him back, even though he is just lying to my side, his one arm wrapped tight across my middle, holding me tight to him. The breeze that hits my exposed skin makes him feel a mile away.

His movement next to me draws my attention to him.

He points in the direction of the lake. "Look across the lake."

Looking across the water, I spot what he is seeing. Three deer, a fawn and her twin does, drinking from the lake. It's beautiful and even though I would love to lie here, naked with Asher, I want to take a picture of the sight before us as well.

I untangle myself from Asher and grab the first garment I touch, which ends up being the button-up shirt Asher was wearing. Pulling it on, it hangs long enough, I button a couple of the buttons and search for my jeans, my cell phone is in the pocket.

Finding what I'm searching for, I don't even bother to put my jeans on, I let them fall back to the ground and I walk down to the lake's edge and capture the sight of nature in front of me.

CHAPTER EIGHTEEN

ASHER

Watching as Jordyn makes her way over to the lake, I'm mesmerized more by the sight of her walking away from me than the animals drinking from the water. With each step she takes the back of the shirt rises just enough to tease me with a small view of her naked backside under the hem.

Jordyn, her back to me, is wearing only my shirt, which is sexier than anything I've ever seen. She looks over her shoulder a couple of times, her smile and excitement shining all around her. This is the image that will be burned into my memory. Right next to the look in her eyes when she gave herself to me just moments ago.

Never have I felt this connected to a woman before. Of course, there has never been anyone like Jordyn either. I'm no saint, but I'm not a player either. I just don't sleep around because I'm popular and women are throwing themselves at me. There have been relationships in my past, but only a handful at the most.

I believe that love has its own timeline. For some the connection can be instant, others it may take a little longer. The moment I saw her stumble over the stool in the sound room and the embarrassment that instantly colored her cheeks, something tugged at my heart. Then she sang, and I thought my knees were going to give out under me. There is also the moment she taught me to feel the music when she was over at my house the other day. The look in her eyes when we found our release together just a few moment ago, and now this sight before me. This woman has completely taken over my soul. I'll do anything to keep seeing that smile that she has at this moment.

Grabbing my jeans, I slide them on and walk over, wrapping my arms around her waist and pulling her back against my chest. Her phone comes up and I see the two of us on her screen as her camera is now pointing at us.

With both of our faces in the camera, I know she can see my lips. "I think my shirt looks a whole lot better on you, than me."

She bends her head back and tilts her lips up for a kiss. I can hear the faint sound of the phone capturing the image of us kissing as I take the sweet lips she is offering me.

Turning herself in my arms, she says, "Thank you for today. This is perfect."

"Well, it's the only place I could think of that we could stand half-naked, and not have the images appear on social media in the morning."

"Oh, so your only plan was to get me naked?" she asks, playfully pushing away from my chest.

My arms tighten around her. "Planned, no! Hopeful, not going to lie, absolutely."

Her phone vibrates in her hand against my chest. Looking down, her eyes widen at whatever has been sent over.

"Scott just emailed me the schedule." The smile in her eyes is replaced with something else. I wouldn't say fear, but maybe a little panic.

"Let me see." She tilts the phone so that I can see the email.

It's a calendar, and starting tomorrow it's full until we leave for the festival next week. Photoshoots, studio time, interviews, salon dates, there is even a shopping date.

"Why would I have to schedule shopping? Megan is going to love that part of the schedule."

"Megan is your best friend, right?"

"Yes, and now assistant. I figured she was perfect for the job, Scott and I chatted a little about it yesterday. My mom actually brought up the subject when I was at their house yesterday about having an interpreter, it just so happens that her job now is an assistant, and of course she signs, so who better to take the job? She is meeting with Scott tomorrow, as a matter of fact. I set it up on the drive out here through emails this morning."

Her eyes fall to the schedule once again, she takes a deep breath as I watch her eyes scan the screen.

Pulling her phone out of her hand, I tuck it into my back pocket. "Let's not worry about the schedule for today. We both knew things were going to get busy, Scott made that very clear yesterday, that's why I picked this place today. A little peace and quiet before the craziness of Scott begins."

She nods, but I can still see a trace of nervousness in her eyes. "I have a favor to ask."

"What kind of favor?" Her fingers trace small circles on my bare chest.

"I want you to teach me some sign language."

Her fingers stop, and now there is shock replacing the nervousness in her eyes. "Really?"

"Why do you look so surprised?"

"I'm sorry, it's just that no one has ever asked me to teach them sign language before."

That starts questions about past relationships flying through my head. Has her past boyfriends been deaf, or just selfish and not caring to learn a little of her world?

"Well then, I would like to be your first student. I want to adapt to your world so that you don't have to always adapt only to mine."

"Asher, I have already adapted."

"Jordyn, watching you sign is amazing to me. I want to learn. Please, will you teach me sign language?"

CHAPTER NINETEEN

JORDYN

If Asher hadn't already stolen my heart, this moment would have sealed it. I haven't had many relationships, two to be exact, but neither one of them ever showed any interest in learning to sign.

Since becoming deaf, I've learned to adapt to what I no longer have. My parents, brother and Megan all learned to sign as I was learning. Mr. Emly learned on his own. Those were the most important people in my life and they all adapted with me to help me learn to accept what I had lost. Honestly, with my past relationships, it never occurred to me that they weren't willing to learn. Now that Asher has asked, I realize why those relationships wouldn't have worked.

"Let me know when you want to start, and I'll be happy to teach you to sign."

"I think the sooner the better. How about now?" Grabbing my hand, he leads us back to the blanket and sits down.

I can't help but laugh at the boyish look of excitement shining all over his face right now. I sit down in front of him, still only wearing his shirt, him bare-chested and only wearing his jeans.

"What would you like to start with?"

"You are the teacher, you tell me."

"I'm thinking we start with the alphabet. That way you can at least spell words, until you learn the sign for them."

For the next thirty minutes we work on the simple part of the language. I'm surprised on how fast he picks it up and I can't help but smile at the seriousness his face holds while he learns. He is very concentrated on what my hands do and he repeats every movement I make.

"Wow, you're a fast learner. I'm impressed."

He rolls his eyes, "Jordyn, you have taught me my ABCs. How does one get impressed over something we learned in kindergarten?"

"Asher, learning a new language isn't easy regardless if those ABCs are with your hands or a different speaking language." When he doesn't look convinced of what I'm saying, I decide to move him to words. " Fine, what would you like to learn to say first?"

I watch as his facial features change as he thinks about what he wants to learn to say. He goes from sarcastic, to a softer look in his eyes as they hold mine. "You have captured my heart."

This is the second time he has told me this, but the way his eyes are holding mine right now, something else is there that he is holding off from saying.

With each sign I make, he mimics with his own hands.

I show him a couple of times. I begin to show him one more time when he stops my hands. Leaning forward, he takes my lips in one of the sweetest kisses we have shared. Pulling back, his hands begin to move. He is signing what I just taught him, but not just to repeat it, his eyes tell me he means it.

Getting up onto my knees, I move myself to straddle his lap. I don't want the distance between us anymore. I can't put into words, or sign, my feelings for him. There is nothing that would express fully enough how he makes me feel. My fingers weave into the hair at the back of his head and I seek his lips out with mine. His fingers instantly go to the buttons at the front of his shirt that I'm wearing and before I know it, he has them unbuttoned and I'm pressed skin to skin up against his chest. His hand now on my bare backside is holding me close to him. I can feel his hardness against me and once again the need to have him inside of me is about to have me already coming completely undone.

Bringing my hands around and against the warm skin of his chest, I push him back, using a different language to express what I want. He looks up at me and I see the blue fire of his eyes take me in. I'm straddled above him, his shirt opened exposing all of me to his eyes. His hands come up, each cupping one of my breasts. I sit there and let him have his moment because this time I'm the one who is going to be doing the pleasuring.

Watching his eyes flare brighter as he takes my nipples and pinches them between his finger and thumb, my breath catches and they harden to a tight bud. I find myself arching my back, begging him for more. As one hand continues its play on my breast, his other hand begins a journey down the valley between my breasts, over my stomach, to the heated center between my legs. I'm trying very hard to keep the control right now, but he is making that very difficult.

Quickly pulling away from his touch is hard, but if I want to have my time pleasuring him, I need to stop his hands from their torturous journey. I push myself back along his legs enough to give me room to run my tongue around each tight nipple, while my hands work on the buttons of his jeans. I push myself down his legs as my tongue travels along each muscle of his abs. My hands at the waistband of his jeans, I begin to pull them down, and Asher lifts his hips to help me as I slide his jeans down. Rocking back on my heels, I finish removing the only clothing he is wearing.

I sit up to let his shirt fall from my arms, but he sits up quickly, his hand shooting out and stopping me, keeping the shirt in place. "Keep it on."

My hand placed on his chest, I push him back as I make my way back up his body, my lips finding his for a quick and very heated kiss. I want his lips on my breast. I pull myself up just enough to bring my chest to his lips, a silent invite of what I'm wanting. He understands completely as he captures one begging tight nipple into his mouth and sucks, hard.

I rock slightly and can feel his hardness brush against my throbbing core and I almost forget what I was planning on doing and just take him deep inside me now.

Moving myself back, Asher has no choice but to release the hold his mouth has and his eyes instantly search mine for what is happening. Our eyes lock as I slowly make my way once again down his chest, my hand wraps around his hardness and I watch as Asher's eyes cloud over to an almost a white-blue with my touch. My thumb rubs over the tip, finding the slight bead of moisture, and as I rub it across the tip, his eyes close.

His eyes fly open at the first touch of my tongue against the underside of his hardness. They lock with mine as I run my tongue up to the tip. His fingers are now tangled into my long hair, his fingers digging into my scalp.

I take him fully into my mouth and his hips thrust forward. I slowly suck my way to the tip, my tongue running along the underside the whole way, and then take him fully into my mouth once again.

His head shakes no, and I feel his hand pulling my hair. His manhood pops from my lips. Asher sits up, grabs my arms and pulls me back up to him.

"I want to lose myself inside of you, not your mouth. I need to be inside of you now."

He lifts me easily by the waist and brings me down onto his hardness, instantly filling me completely as his lips make work on one very tight nipple of my breast. My head falls back, my back thrusting my chest forward, begging him for more.

His hands on my hips begin to move me. Slowly out, hard thrust back, bringing him deeper and deeper inside of me each time. Between that sensation and the way his tongue is playing with my breast, my body begins to shake.

Asher's exploration of my breast ends and his eyes

look up into mine. "Take me fully in, Jordyn. I feel your body pulling me deeper."

His hands move my hips faster and faster and I can no longer hold back. I fall apart around him. His arms wrap tight around my waist as my body pulls him deeper and deeper inside of me with each wave of release I have. I feel his chest rumble against mine, his arms tighten and I know he has found his release as well.

I'm not sure how long we sit here, holding each other tightly, but I have no desire to move.

I watch as we pass by the meadows leaving the lake. The sun is setting and leaving the whole area cast in a mixture of golds and reds from the reflection. I'm not ready to leave the lake. It means tomorrow is that much closer. I'm excited and terrified. I've dreamt of being on stage my whole life, but I'm not naive, the chances of a deaf girl getting to live out that dream was slim to none. I smile to myself, leave it to Mr. Emly to find a way.

Speaking of Mr. Emly, I pull my phone out and look through text messages I have missed throughout the day. The only texts I have received from him is a quick one telling me he is proud of me after I texted him telling him I'd signed on with the group.

Asher's hand grabs mine, bringing my attention to him. "Are you all right? There is a lot of sighing going on from over there." He looks down at my phone in hand with a questioning look.

Pressing the button on the side of the phone turning it off, I set it in my lap. "Sorry, I was just checking. I haven't heard much from Mr. Emly, and I thought there would be more of a response from him."

"He stopped by my house yesterday."

My eyes round with surprise. I can't get him to message me back and he went to Asher's house? "Why?"

Asher shrugs, "Well, like your brother, I'm thinking he was concerned about the image floating around the internet and making sure that I'm worthy."

His smile strikes me right in the heart. He is being very understanding with the protective men in my life. "I'm sorry. First my brother and then Mr. Emly."

"I'll be honest, kind of surprised I haven't heard from your dad."

"Trust me, he and Justin had a conversation yesterday. My dad isn't really a talk over the phone kind of guy. He'll wait until he meets you in person, but he won't wait long."

"Should we stop by there tonight? Might as well meet everyone now. With the announcement getting ready to happen, there's no way of telling what way the social media platforms are going to spin our relationship. I'd rather your parents know me before they see any more pictures of me making out with their daughter on the internet."

"I'm sure my father would appreciate it if there weren't any images of us making out on the Internet at all, but I agree, it would be better if they met you before anymore images hit the news."

Megan is already taking her assistant job very seriously and has texted over my schedule, which I already have, but I didn't have the heart to tell her that. She and Scott met up today. She has officially accepted the job and is in full swing assistant mode. I start first thing tomorrow morning with a hair appointment and makeup, to be ready for the photoshoot tomorrow afternoon and then following those the interviews.

Megan used her position as my interpreter with her current job to convince them to allow her to work remotely for the next couple of weeks. They agreed, but added that she has to find her replacement. If I know anything about my best friend, she'll have someone hired in two days, have them trained by the end of the week, and free and clear by the weekend.

"If you are really wanting to meet them, I can text and make sure they are home."

"I would rather them know me a little before it gets out to everyone else."

After a couple quick messages between my mom and myself, it's confirmed, we'll be having dinner with my parents, brother and sister-in-law. Have to admit, I'm a little nervous.

Sitting in my parents' driveway, I watch as Asher rounds the front of the truck and comes to open my door. When I don't move right away to step down from my seat, his eyes shift a little.

"Are you all right with all of this? I understand if you think this is all moving a little fast. Only problem right now is, we are parked in front of the house, it may give them the idea that I chickened out if we leave, but I can take it."

I can't help but laugh. He seems so laid back, so sure.

He doesn't look nervous at all. I think I'm nervous enough for the both of us.

"I'm not going to lie, everything the past weekend has made my head spin a little. Joining the group, having my picture fly around the internet. You."

CHAPTER TWENTY

ASHER

I place my hand on her knee, turning her body and placing myself between her legs. Looking up into her eyes, her nerves are shining back at me. "I didn't mean to push you into having me meet your parents tonight, Jordyn. I just thought it would be best if they met me before the media slides into our lives."

"Asher, it's been five days, most women fear asking the guy in their life too early to meet their parents, afraid to scare them off."

This is when I see it. She isn't nervous about me meeting her parents, she is nervous about how I see the relationship between the two of us.

"Jordyn, I've never been one of those guys that is shy. I can find words to speak what is on my mind and in my heart and I'm not embarrassed or nervous about voicing them. I'm not a player and I've no intention on dating lots of women because I can. I want the real thing. You captured my heart the moment I saw you in the studio. I'll admit, I'm a little nervous, but only because I fear what everything at once is going to do to you. I want to be that rock you hold on to when the world seems like it is sliding a little too fast downhill. It will happen, I've been there, but I've already witnessed your strength and I think you are going to be great."

Taking her hand, I place it on my chest above my heart. "It's yours, Jordyn, that beat is our song."

Her fingers fist into my shirt, and she pulls me up to meet her lips. It's a soft kiss and I keep my hands on her knees to assure I keep from pulling her to me and deepening the kiss. It probably wouldn't look good to her parents if they saw us making out in their driveway.

She pulls away from me and smiles, "So what you are telling me is that I'm stuck with you."

"Yes, ma'am."

"All right, then let's go and introduce you to my parents."

Taking a step back, I give her some room to step down and out of the truck. Shutting her door, she grabs my hand and leads the way.

The front door is pulled open before we make it to the porch. A woman steps out to meet us, her hands flying as she steps out.

"Mom, enough." Jordyn shakes her head at the woman.

Jordyn looks exactly like her mom, same build, hair color, only difference are the eyes. Before I can ask what she said, she walks right up to me and wraps me in a hug.

"Mrs. Collins, it's a pleasure to meet you."

"Please, call me Jessica." Turning, she points to a man

who, no doubt, is Jordyn's father. Now I completely understand where her brother gets his height and she gets her eyes. "This is Jordyn's father, Joseph."

I reach out a hand, "Mr. Collins, it's nice to meet you."

He accepts my handshake, squeezing a lot harder than need be, but I didn't expect anything different. His little girl, famous country singer, he is testing me, but my dad brought us up to respond the same, to prove to the father you are capable of taking care of his little girl, but not able to take the place of her daddy.

For a moment it's a test. I keep eye contact, and show no signs of nerves. It takes a little time, but I finally see the slightest of smiles from the man and his hand releases mine. "Asher, nice to meet you."

"Come on in, guys," Jessica places a hand on my back and ushers us into the house. Leaning into me, she says, "You can call him Joe."

"Mr. Collins will be good for now," the large man turns in front of us and leads the way into the house.

"Pay him no attention."

"Dad, be nice."

Both Mrs. Collins and Jordyn speak at the same time.

Laughing, I get it. "It's all good," I reassure Jordyn when she gives me the apologetic eyes for her dad.

Jordyn and I are led through the house by her mother, followed by her father, and into the living room. As we enter, her brother stands from the couch, cradling a little girl in one giant arm. A gentle giant.

"Justin, good to see you again." I reach out to shake his hand.

"Asher, this my wife, Amber, and our little girl, Kylie."

Amber extends her hand out to me, "Asher, it's nice to meet you. I've heard a lot."

"Nice to meet you. Your little one is beautiful."

"Dinner is ready, come on, everyone, into the dining room. We can talk more there" Mrs. Collins announces as she disappears through a doorway to what looks like would be the kitchen.

Following Jordyn into the dining room, the smell of lasagna instantly takes over my senses. Her mom has gone all out.

Everyone takes a seat and I notice Justin still has a tight hold on his daughter. It's great to see such a large man trying to look tough with such an adorable little girl. He gives his wife just as much attention, as he waits for her to be seated first.

I follow Jordyn to the opposite side of the table and wait as Jordyn takes her seat. It doesn't go unnoticed the small smile her dad shows when I wait for her to sit first. My dad raised me to be a gentleman and it's giving me points with her father.

Once the food has been passed around and plates are full, the questions begin.

"So, Asher, how long have you and your band been together?" Mrs. Collins starts the conversation.

"Since high school. We've all been friends for years, though. Then there is my brother, Noah."

"What made you guys decide you needed to add to the group, aren't you guys doing pretty good?" Amber's turn.

"Actually that was all our manager's idea. He thinks adding a female voice is going to take us over the top. I'll be honest, we weren't sure of the idea at first. Most of us have been together for years and the band is doing great with just us guys."

"That opinion has changed now?" Mr. Collins sets a strong pair of eyes on me.

"When I headed into the studio last week, I figured I'd humor Scott, our manager, and show up so I could tell him it wasn't going to work. The moment I walked into the room, Jordyn had me mesmerized."

"I knocked over everything in the sound room." Jordyn's cheeks instantly brighten.

"Yes, you did, but then you sang. I've never heard a voice like yours. I found myself singing along with you and something clicked. It felt right. Jordyn brings something different to music."

"And the rest of the group, how do they feel about her being brought in?" Mr. Collins continues with the questions.

"Everyone is excited to have her join. We are a large family and I guess the best way to put it is you can never have too much family, sir."

Setting down his fork onto his plate, Mr. Collins takes a moment, wiping his mouth with his napkin. When he sets it down into his lap, he looks me square in the eyes, "This image that is floating around?"

Looking over at Jordyn at my side, I make sure she understands every word I tell her father. "Yes, sir. I'm not sorry that I was caught kissing your daughter, but I am sorry it was splashed across social media like it was and I can't say it won't happen again. Your daughter has captured a part of me that no one else has. This isn't something that is going to go away either. It's only been what, five days, and I can't predict the future, but what I can tell you is that I've no plans on hiding how I feel about her, or trying to hide what we have together from the media world like a dark secret. It's going to get a little insane and probably a whole lot of crazy, but we have talked about it and we're going to go into it together."

"Dad, I know you and Justin worry about me. I know the difference the world is to me from everyone else, but I'm an adult and I can take care of myself, despite what you and Justin may think sometimes. Plus, Meghan just signed on with the group as my translator and PA. It's going to be fine."

"Jordyn, I've been around this industry for a while now. I know what the paparazzi can do..."

Jordyn cuts her brother off, "Yes, and I'm not alone."

Brother and sister lock eyes. I see the worry in Justin's and understand it. Jordyn's eyes hold a determination but I also see an understanding spark in them.

"All right, you two, enough," Mrs. Collins breaks the silence around the table, her hands are up as she speaks. "Jordyn, your brother is only concerned, it's his job in more ways than one. We're very proud of you and excited for your new adventure. This is something you have always wanted and despite what has been taken from you, you've been determined to fulfill your dreams. Asher, please know that Jordyn has become part of your family and you have become a part of ours."

"Thank you, Mrs. Collins."

"Well, maybe not if you don't stop calling me Mrs. Collins."

"Yes, ma'am."

The rest of the dinner conversation is filled with questions about the upcoming concert at the Country Stampede. It doesn't go unnoticed how quiet Justin has become. I know there are no words I can say to him to assure him Jordyn is in safe hands, but I have an idea that might possibly make things a little easier, but it's something I need to run by Scott and Jordyn first before I say anything to him. I see how she is trying to separate and become a little more independent and having her brother's overprotective ways may be something she is trying to break away from.

It's almost eleven by the time I pull into Jordyn's apartment complex. We have a busy day tomorrow and hers starts way earlier than mine.

Walking her up to her door, she opens it and turns to me, "Do you want to come in for a little while?"

As much as I'd love to spend a couple more hours with her, we both need rest. "I'd love to, yes, but you have an early morning and tomorrow is going to be a little crazy, you should get some rest."

Nodding, she grabs the front of my shirt and pulls my lips down to hers. This isn't making it easy for me to leave. I grab the framing of the door to keep from pushing her inside and forgetting about going home.

Giving her all control, I'm pretty sure I'm about to lose the battle, when she pulls away, ending the kiss.

"I'll see you tomorrow afternoon."

Nodding, I give her one last quick kiss and wait for her to shut her front door before heading back to my truck.

CHAPTER TWENTY-ONE

JORDYN

Dropping my bag on the kitchen counter, I walk straight into my room and flop down onto my bed, what a day. Lying back, I grab a pillow and hug it tight. I kind of feel like a school girl, all excited after the first date and the first kiss goodnight, only it went so much further than just the first kiss.

Brushing a finger over my lips, I still feel Asher's lips on mine. They have been there most of the day. Smiling to myself, I think back to the lake. His hands on my body, the way he looked at me. Girls dream of a guy looking at her as if she is his world, and I'm living that dream.

I know how fast a person's life can change, I've lived it. In a matter of moments my world was flipped upside down with that car accident. One minute I was talking to my family, listening to the music from the radio in the background, the next nothing but silence.

Today at the lake as I looked around, I tried to imagine what everything sounded like from memories that I'm not even sure are correct any more it's been so long. As I stood there I imagined the music each part of nature would be creating and even though I was probably way off, the music in my head was beautiful.

Every movement of Asher's lips as he talks to me makes me wish I could hear his voice. I've tried to imagine what it sounds like, deep, smooth and probably with a little southern accent.

My phone vibrates in my back pocket reminding me that I've ignored a few text messages this evening.

Rolling to my side, I grab it from my pocket, pushing the button on the side to wake it up. Several texts, all from Megan.

Megan: How was your date?

Megan: Are you home yet? I need details.

Megan: We need to talk about tomorrow.

Megan: Why are you ignoring me?

Megan: HELLO!!!

The last text came though about forty-five minutes ago. I have to say, I'm surprised she stopped.

Me: Just got home.

It's late, but I knew she would be awake. Her response was almost instant.

Megan: Well happy to see you are alive. Why the silent treatment?

I laugh, she has always been a little overdramatic at times, but it's one of the reasons why I love her so much.

Me: Sorry, It's been a busy day.

Megan: Am I getting any of the details?

Me: Not over text.

Megan: Fine, I'll be at your house at 8:00, I expect

details. Don't worry about hair and makeup in the morning before we leave, that is what the salon appointment in the morning is for.

That tingly feeling that shoots up your body like a cold chill rocks my body, it's pure excitement, this is really happening.

Photoshoots, interviews, practice schedule, new songs to learn, group meetings, recording session, it is something every day for the next week and a half. The schedule is crazy up until we leave for the Country Stampede next Wednesday. Scott has packed the schedule tight.

I hope I'm everything they are thinking I am, I'm just worried about letting everyone down, especially Mr. Emly. That there is a whole new worry. I really haven't heard anything from him since the night we went out to dinner with the band. Asher made the comment that he had stopped by his house, but all I'm getting is a couple word responses on the text messages I've sent out and that isn't like him. I'm thinking I'm going to have to stop by and see him, make him tell me what's going on.

Looking at the clock on my phone, it's almost midnight and starting a photoshoot off with exhausted looking eyes probably isn't the best way to set a good first impression.

Sitting up, I take a couple deep breaths and tell myself to relax. I have Megan with me and even though I know I'm able to communicate just fine on my own, it's a nice feeling knowing I have her there just in case. I don't want me being deaf to be the main focus of the new singer who joined the band, I'd rather have people just like me for my voice, not the amazing factor that my ears don't work but I can still sing. I think that is my worst fear in all of this. Not being known as one of the members of Driven Roads, but being known as the deaf singer. I want to be an equal member of the group, not the extra attention because of my disability.

"Knock it off, Jordyn," I scold myself. Getting up from the bed, I walk over and grab a pair of sleep shorts and tank top out of my dresser and head for the bathroom. I need to just go with the flow and decide on how to handle situations as they happen. No reason worrying over stuff and getting all worked up. My inability to hear isn't something I can or want to hide. I'm not ashamed and I've worked hard to get where I want to be, that's my main focus. I silently lecture myself through the mirror.

The lights throughout the house flash at exactly eight. Rushing to the door, I open it to find Megan, head down looking at her phone, standing there right on time.

She looks up and gives me a once over. "Why are you still in your pajamas? I said I would be here at eight," she signs.

"I have no idea what to wear."

Watching her shoulders relax a little, she pushes her way through the door, shutting it behind her. "Just put something causal on, they will have the wardrobe for the shoot, you just can't wear that," she waves her hand in front of me referring to my very short sleeping shorts and tank top.

"Okay, give me a minute." Turning, I make my way back to my room, quickly grabbing a pair of jeans and a plain short-sleeve top.

Turning back around, she startles me when I see her sitting on my bed, I didn't even know she followed me into the room.

"So let's hear it. How was your date with Asher yesterday?"

"It was great. We went to this lake he went to a lot growing up, had a nice lunch, talked..."

"Talked and had lunch, that's all you did?" she interrupts me with a questioning look on her face.

"We kissed," I added, making my way to the bathroom to change.

Placing my clothes on the counter, I look in the mirror to find my friend has followed me once again.

"And..."

"And what?"

"Jordyn, I don't know who you think you are fooling but those red cheeks of yours are telling me you did more than just kiss," her hands are exaggerated as she signs.

I have no idea why I even try hiding anything from her, she knows me too well.

Turning to face her, I give in, "Fine, there was more than just kissing. Before you ask, yes, it was amazing and no, you are not getting the details."

"I don't want the exact detail, knowing it was good is enough. You do realize you had sex with Asher James, right?"

I shake my head at my friend's excitement over my sex life. "Yes, Megan, I know who I had sex with. Now, can you give me a little privacy to get dressed?"

"Hurry up, we need to get going," she scolds and then turns and walks out of the bathroom.

. . .

Ten minutes later we are heading out the door, my nerves kicking in a little more with each step we take down to the parking lot.

Megan stops halfway down the stairs and turns to me, "I need to make a call to my replacement, so can you drive?" Megan is already scrolling through her phone before I can answer.

I'm more than happy to drive, it gives me something else to set my attention on instead of just sitting in the passenger seat with more time to think.

In between her conversation on the phone, she signs to me which direction to turn. Megan is in full work mode and it amazes me how well she can multitask. She may be my crazy, over-exaggerating, sometimes a little 'over the top' best friend, but when she is in work mode she is all professional and organized.

Pulling into the parking lot of the salon, Megan ends her call, and puts her attention on me. "We have an appointment here for hair, then we head to the studio for makeup before the shoot."

Nodding is all I have time for before she's out the passenger side of my car and heading to the front door of the salon. Quickly turning off the engine to my Jeep, I sit here for a moment and take a deep breath. Let's do this.

Three hours I've been sitting in this chair, while they've colored my hair, trimmed it and are now styling for the photos. The whole time Megan has been on the phone with the new girl she hired to take her place at her last job. I knew when I asked her to take this job she was the right one to ask to do it.

When the two of us are together, we get to let ourselves go a little. She is night and day from her work self to her everyday self. Megan doesn't let what other people may think of her keep her from doing what makes her happy or from having fun. I'm a little more reserved of the two of us, she puts herself out there, I stand back behind the crowd and watch. We are complete opposites but I think that's what makes this friendship amazing.

I can see her in the mirror behind me, she is finally off the phone. She takes a couple of deep breaths.

"Everything all right?"

She stands from the chair and walks over to stand in front of me, "Yes, I just want to get the new girl trained so I can put all my concentration here. She is learning fast, but when you have to transfer everything and get her into the groove of what the office is used to working with, it takes a little time."

"I hope you don't have any regrets."

"Are you kidding? I get to travel with my best friend. I think this is definitely the better of the two choices."

"I know it's more about the hot guys than anything else, but I'm excited to have you with me."

"Hot guys are just the extra bonus, being with you is the best part." Looking down at her phone, I watch as her playful expression turns back to professional. "Not to rush perfection or anything, but we have to get a move on," she reminds the stylist putting the finishing touches on my hair.

. . .

Finally finished with my hair, we are now on our way to the studio for the photoshoot. With each fast food place we pass, I beg Megan to let me stop. This morning I didn't eat much, my nerves were getting the best of me, and now Megan is telling me we don't have time.

"Look, let's just get to the studio and get you settled into makeup. I'll go out and grab you something while your makeup is being done," Megan signs when I give her a pleading look after probably the tenth place we have passed.

Realizing I have no choice, I keep going. Lesson learned, pack a couple snacks just in case the schedule doesn't allow for food stops.

Scott is outside and it looks like on his phone when we pull up to the studio. He waves and the butterflies that had finally settled while getting my hair done have returned with friends. Pulling into a parking spot, I see Scott hang up his phone and walk out to meet us, opening the driver's door for me just as I turn the ignition off.

"Perfect timing, ladies. Everyone is set up inside and the guys should be here shortly. Food is set up and you have a little time to grab something if you are hungry."

Megan comes around the front of the Jeep and she and Scott start walking off in front of me, both chatting back and forth. I have no idea what they are saying, but right now I really don't care, he mentioned food and I'm starving.

Once inside, I follow Scott down a hallway into a large studio. Stations are set up for makeup, dressing screens are spread out, and a large area is set up with flashes. We stop at a table filled with sandwiches, fruit, bottles of water, chips, pretzels and crackers.

Scott turns to me, "Go ahead and help yourself, I'm going to steal Megan for a moment and give her a rundown of tomorrow's interviews. You good?"

"Yes, I'll be fine," I assure him and Megan, who looks hesitant to leave me but ends up following Scott as he walks away.

Looking around, I notice no one else is eating and even though I could easily fill a plate with everything on the table, I feel weird being the only one eating.

As I watch everyone around me hustle around finishing last-minute odd jobs to get everything set up, I realize the more I stand here watching their attention is starting to collect on to me. Small groups are looking and talking. Yes, I'm the new face, but this isn't attention because I'm the new member of the group, I catch a couple of them mentioning Asher's name. Good thing about lip reading, you don't have to be standing right next to the person to know what they are saying. I'm catching a little about our picture floating around the social media pages. They are all starting to figure out who I am.

A group of three women about my age catches me attention.

"I was told she is deaf."

"How can she be deaf and be able to sing?"

Their eyes are locked on mine, I have to hide the small smile, it's kind of funny. The one believes I'm deaf, but from her position and the way she is leaning into the other two ladies I can tell she is whispering, as though she doesn't want me to hear her.

Movement to my right catches my attention as Megan joins me again, her hands are moving as she rounds the food table. "Why aren't you eating? I thought you were starving."

Her signing doesn't go unnoticed by the small group, the one that originally made the announcement to the other two points at the two of us, "See, I told you."

Megan grabs a plate and hands it to me, bringing my attention back to her. "If you don't eat now I can't tell you when your next meal will be."

"No one else was eating, I felt weird," I explained.

She starts grabbing from the table, quickly filling her plate, "You are so weird with that whole eating alone in public thing. I'm eating, too, so hurry up."

"You're bossy."

"That's my job."

Glancing back at the three woman, they are all standing there just gawking now. We have switched between signing and talking and they don't know what to make of it, this could be a little fun.

There is more involved with photoshoots than I could ever imagine. Outfit changes and I can't even guess how many layers of makeup I have on my face. If there was a moment the photographer didn't have the camera pointing at us, we had the makeup artists there with their brushes, it was a little insane. I have to admit, though, it was kind of fun, but exhausting. Who would have thought standing still all day could wear a person out?

Arms wrap around me from behind, turning myself to face him, his lips take mine before I can say a word. We haven't had a whole lot of time today so it's a welcoming feeling to be in his arms.

"Do you want to grab a pizza and have a movie night?"

"As tempting as that sounds, I have songs to learn tonight before tomorrow."

"You know, I think I may be able to help you with those."

"You and I both know we wouldn't get much done."

"Are you saying I can't control myself around you?" He tries to look offended.

"I'm saying that I don't think I want you to control yourself, and with that being said, I need to pass on the invitation so that I can get a little work done before I show up tomorrow and make a complete fool of myself."

"I'm pretty sure you already know every one of our songs by heart and probably better than any one of us, but I won't beg, unless you think it would work."

Saying no to Asher has to be one of the hardest things I've ever done, especially with his arms tightly wrapped around me, and his lips making my head go a little foggy with each kiss.

"I've already promised Megan that we will get my schedule ran through tonight, even though I already have it memorized. She is taking her new job pretty serious."

Nodding his head, his eyes look past me, "I'm pretty sure if you wanted me to talk to my brother about asking her out tonight, it wouldn't take much convincing."

Turning to look in the direction that has his attention, I see Megan and Noah. Megan is leaning a little too much into Noah and laughing at something he has said, she is in full flirt mode.

I bring my eyes back to Asher, "As much as I would love to have a movie night with you, I really need to make sure I'm ready for tomorrow."

"Fine, I'll ask my brother on a date."

Laughing, I kiss him once again.

"Just to warn you, I'm not taking no for an answer for tomorrow night," he warns me.

"Tomorrow evening, I'm all yours."

CHAPTER TWENTY-TWO

ASHER

As much as I wanted to spend the evening with Jordyn, I know she is nervous and just trying to make sure she has everything perfect so that she doesn't disappoint anyone.

A pair of hands clamp down onto my shoulders. "Jesse needs to get home and Dawson and Zayden have plans for the evening so Dean and I were going to grab a burger and a beer, want to join us?" My brother's voice comes from behind me.

Sitting at the house will only having me wishing I was with Jordyn, so a burger and a beer sound better than sitting alone, "I'm in."

Nice thing about finding a place to eat that you go to a lot is that yes, we still get looks and every once in a while a person coming up to the table for a picture or an autograph, but most of the time we are left to eat our food and enjoy our time. The staff and the manager keep most of it under control.

"I'm thinking from the display of affection today and your inability to not mention Jordyn's name at least every few minutes means that you, my brother, are off the market," Noah takes a drink of his beer.

"It seems a little fast," Dean pops in with his opinion.

"You guys have already had a taste of what social media is going to go after, that isn't going to get better once the announcement tomorrow happens about her being a new member of our group. That's a lot to handle all at once."

Noah isn't telling me anything I haven't already thought about a million times, or that Jordyn and I haven't already talked about.

"We both know all this, Noah, trust me, I even met her parents last night so that way they could know me a little before the pictures started flying all over the internet."

"Wow, already met the parents, that's serious." Dean sits back in his chair, crossing his arms over his chest.

"Look, Asher, I'm not saying I don't understand where you are coming from. Jordyn isn't like most women, just making sure you know what you two are in for."

"One of the reasons I'm here with you guys, I asked if she wanted to grab a pizza and watch a movie, but she is worried about tomorrow and knowing the songs, so she and Megan are working on them tonight. I wasn't going to push it, I want to give her space when she needs it, because this next is probably going to start feeling a little stifling to her once the news gets out and the cameras start following us around everywhere."

"I think we worry more about the paparazzi than we do the fans." Dean takes a bite of his burger.

Dean isn't wrong. I agree with him completely. Our fans will recognize us in public, they'll ask for pictures or for us to sign something, but all in all, they are pretty calm. Those looking for their next paycheck selling the next perfect picture to social media are not so aware of personal space.

"I have to give it to her, watching her the last few times we've all been around each other, I forget she can't hear. She is very aware of her surroundings. It's kind of neat to watch her and Megan sign, though. It's like being able to talk about someone right in front of their face and them having no clue." Only Noah would think that is the best part of signing.

Dean throws a fry at Noah, "Really, man?"

"What, tell me you haven't thought about that."

"Um, no, I haven't. I do have a question, though, and I promise I'm not trying to sound like an ass or anything, but how does she know when to sing? She can't hear the music."

We've already been in the studio with Jordyn, but the guys haven't really asked many questions, I just assumed they were satisfied with the fact that she did everything in good time to the song.

"Actually, she was taught to feel the music. She showed me a little and it's pretty amazing. Gives you a different perspective for music, that's for sure. You almost appreciate it more. We've also worked out a system where I start the song off with a signal to her and then she follows it with a count." I think back to the evening in my home studio.

"Wait, that would mean she has to memorize every songs count at the beginning to know when to start singing." Dean looks at me like I've lost my mind.

"I'm telling you guys, she is amazing."

We have to be at the studio at ten this morning and I'm just about to text Jordyn and ask if she would like me to pick her up and ride over together when a text from her comes through my phone first.

Jordyn: Any way you could come to the studio a little early? I'd feel better if we could run over the songs first before everyone gets here.

Wait, she just said here.

Me: Where are you?

Jordyn: Don't laugh, I'm at the studio, sitting in the parking lot.

Looking at the clock, it's only half past eight.

Me: They don't usually open the doors until around nine.

Jordyn: I've been made aware of that.

Me: I'm on my way

Jordyn: Thank you

It's a little after nine when I pull into the parking lot, parking right next to Jordyn's Jeep. There are a couple cars here now, but she is still sitting in her car.

Stepping out of my truck, I round the back and walk

over to her driver's side door, opening it. "Why are you still sitting out here?"

"I realize my nerves may have gotten the best of me and I might look a little foolish walking in two hours before everyone else in the band."

"First off, it's not foolish. Second, why are you so nervous? You've already sang with the band, it's just a recording day on a couple new songs. Trust me when I say, it probably won't be you messing up today. You probably know the words better than us guys do. Nice thing is we can restart as many times as we need to, and with this group of guys, trust me, there are going to be restarts. It's going to be a long day."

Taking a deep breath, she places her head back against the headrest. "I'm sorry, I don't know what's gotten into me. This isn't like me at all. I'm usually pretty confident when it comes to music and the songs I sing. I think between Megan and all the texted over schedules and Justin getting into my head, I'm freaking myself out."

Grabbing her hand, I pull her out of the Jeep, shutting her door. "Listen, it really isn't that bad. Right now, yes, it seems like everything is in hyper speed because it's being thrown at you all at once. In a few days it will seem like just a regular work schedule. Our job is just more fun than most. As for Justin, he is just worried, he has been around this world and so many others in the industry and you are his little sister. Deaf or not, he would worry."

Leaning back against the Jeep, she nods. "You're right. I'm sorry to have had you come here so early."

"Let's make the most out of it." I point to the diner

across the street, "They have amazing breakfast, why don't we go and grab something to eat?"

We are taking a ten-minute break when Scott comes through the door, holding his phone up to the glass between us and the control room, showing us the image on it. "Well, it's noon and official. The announcement was just made, pictures are flying all over social media from yesterday's photoshoot. Jordyn, you are officially a member of Driven Roads."

All at once everyone pulls out their phones and like Scott said, it's already soaring through social media. Not only the images from yesterday's shoot, but side by sides of the original image of Jordyn and me kissing in the parking lot. Captions reading, "Is the new member of Driven Roads Asher's new mystery girl?"

Jordyn turns her phone screen to me which has the same image I am looking at. "It begins."

"It's all good, we've got this," I reassure her.

"This is why I have the interviews set up for tomorrow," Scott announces. "We don't hide from it, it only feeds them more. Make your announcements to the public, that way there is no mystery and they move on a little faster."

"It's kind of crazy seeing these images from yesterday and me in them," Jordyn changes the subject.

"Now that the images are live, I hope you know that means you are stuck with us," Jesse teases.

"Well, according to Scott's plan, some girl had to do it, I guess it may as well be me," Jordyn comes back quickly.

"Well, Scott's plan now is to have at least one of these songs releasing tomorrow during one of the interviews, so can we please get back to work?" Scott is speaking in the third person, and waves us all back to work as he leaves the room altogether.

"Wow, it will release that quick?" Jordyn's eyes are round with shock.

"If there is one thing about Scott you will learn, it's everything is done on a quick schedule. I can guarantee he had all of this lined up before you even signed the papers, including these two new songs," Noah states.

"He already told me he wasn't waiting for me to write two new songs, that mine would still be included on the new album but he couldn't wait for me," I inform the group.

"Come on, guys, let's get this second song done, my wife informed me today that I have to go shopping with her tonight for Jayline's party this weekend, which by the way, Jordyn, it would be great to have you there," Jesse invites.

CHAPTER TWENTY-THREE

JORDYN

I see Jesse get up and notice the guys are following so I begin to follow, assuming I missed something and we are getting back to work. Jesse stops and turns his attention to me but doesn't say anything. The look on his face is as though he is waiting on me to say something. I definitely believe I missed something.

I look over at Asher with a questioning, or more like a pleading look.

"Jesse, you can't have your back to her if you are going to talk to her," Asher explains to Jesse. He looks at me, "He invited you to his daughter's first birthday party this weekend."

Looking around, everyone is looking at me, and I feel my cheeks starting to heat up from embarrassment. I told Megan she didn't need to come today, I didn't see a reason for it, I see now I might have been wrong. I try and be as independent as possible. I've wanted everyone to see that I'm capable of doing things on my own.

"Shit, sorry, Jordyn." Jesse this time makes sure he is looking right at me.

Shaking my head, I wave him off like it's no big deal.

"We would love to have you join us this weekend, see if Megan would like to come as well," Jesse invites me again.

I thinking the sudden invitation for Megan is to make it easier on me. I'm not sure if I appreciate it or am more embarrassed that he thought of inviting her.

"I don't think Noah would have any complaints if she was there," Jesse continues and now everyone starts laughing and the attention is taken over to Noah, thankfully.

I don't know about how Noah would feel about it, but listening to Megan talk about him all night last night, I'm pretty sure she would be more than willing to come with me.

It takes us about another hour and half to wrap up the second song. Grabbing my stuff, I pull out my phone and it has text messages from everyone. I start flipping through them and it's all over the excitement my family has about the pictures and the announcement of me joining the group. It doesn't go unnoticed, though, that my brother hasn't sent me anything.

Asher walks over to me, taking my bag and reaching for my hand. "Want to go grab that pizza tonight?"

We have interviews scheduled for tomorrow, but there isn't anything that needs to be done before those, plus I did promise him yesterday that tonight we could have a date night. "That sounds great."

Together we walk out of the recording studio and into the main lobby of the building. Nothing surprises me more than finding my brother, standing against the wall, his arms crossed over his chest.

Asher looks over at me with the same questioning look that I have. My brother pushes off the wall when he spots the two of us.

"Justin, what are you doing here?" I ask.

His attention is on Asher instead of me, "I thought you said you guys have security around you."

"We haven't gone anywhere today. We don't usually have them around when we are working in the studio, this place has their own security," Asher points at a couple of guys standing by the front door.

Justin points to the two guards, "Yeah, their job is to keep those they don't want in, out. Their job doesn't include you guys after you leave the building."

That's when I see it. On the other side of the glass doors is a huge group of people, with cameras, waiting.

"Did your agent not think that after making the announcement today that you may need to have a little extra help with those guys?" Justin points to the large group.

"Justin, I get what you are saying but she isn't alone, I'm with her," Asher assures my brother, but Justin doesn't look convinced.

"They're going to swamp you two the moment you step out that door..."

"Stop, Justin," I sign, stopping him from saying any more.

"You have no idea what you are about to walk into," Justin signs back.

Taking a deep breath, I try to calm myself before I say something I know I really don't want to. My brother isn't trying to be the pain I'm finding him to be the last couple of days. I know he's only worried and wants to protect me. After the little missed conversation earlier in the studio with Jesse, and that was minor, it did make me realize I'm going to miss things.

The photographers outside are going to push and shove, there are going to be a lot of things said I'm going to miss. Sure, Asher and I are going out together, but his attention will be pulled in every direction.

The rest of the guys have joined us now. I see them all asking questions, and my brother and Asher responding, but I have no idea what any of them are saying. This is all insane. I've allowed my nerves to get the best of me. I've allowed everyone to get into my head, including the photographers and reporters outside.

Releasing Asher's hand, I take a step outside of the group. "Everyone, stop!"

All eyes turn to me, no one's mouth is moving. "Look, if I'm going to be a part of this group and add to it Asher's girlfriend, all of this," I wave my hand to the people waiting for us outside, "is something I'm going to have to get used to."

Turning my attention to my brother, I continue, "Justin, I love you and I appreciate how hard you work at keeping me safe. I'll admit that I'm glad you are here, but you need to quit questioning everything this group does when it comes to security and protection. Scott isn't going to allow anyone to get hurt, and these guys aren't new to this either."

"If we go out together, we can push through them pretty fast, you know the whole 'safer in numbers' thing," Noah suggests.

Everyone laughs, something this situation needs right now.

Enough is enough, we can't stand here all night wondering how we should proceed in leaving. "Guys, enough. We are going to walk out there and deal with the cameras and you guys will deal with the questions if you choose to. Good thing about being deaf, it's easy to ignore people."

"I'm going with you," Justin dares me to argue as he stares me straight in the eye.

"I wasn't expecting any different, but we are going to talk about this later."

Taking Asher's hand once again, Justin positions himself directly in front of me and the rest of the guys flank us.

Have to admit seeing the group of people outside and them starting to crowd closer as we approach the door, flashes already going off, is a little scary, but exciting at the same time.

My brother is a very large man, but I swear he seems even larger as we walk out the door. I've never seen him in action as he is working. I know he is good at what he does, but it's fascinating to see him actually working.

It's a little weird how in broad daylight a flash from

camera can still seem so bright. I'm sure it has to do with the amount of flashes going off all at once but it's not expected. I won't allow myself to cower behind my brother, but I do feel myself tightening my hold on Asher's hand as the group surrounds us.

Looking around, I see the urgency of people trying to get their questions answered, making sure they have the best picture. My world is all silence, and I want nothing more than to know what the sounds are like around me at this moment. I'm sure it feeds into the excitement one feels in this position. People wanting to know who you are, what you are doing, but for me at this moment, it's flashes of light and a lot of faces all yelling silent words.

I follow close behind my brother and I'm noticing no one from the group is stopping or answering any questions. Everyone is just making their way through the crowd as quickly as we are allowed.

CHAPTER TWENTY-FOUR

ASHER

I have to give it to Justin, he knows how to move a crowd. The group follows us out to the parking lot.

"Is that your truck next to Jordyn's Jeep?" Justin yells over his shoulder.

"Yes."

Justin leads us over to the passenger side of my truck and opens the door for this sister.

"My Jeep is right there," Jordyn points in its direction.

"I'll get it home for you, it's better if you leave with Asher for now, just in case you guys are followed by any of these reporters," Justin signs as he speaks.

Jordyn doesn't argue with him, which honestly surprises me a little.

Rounding the front of my truck, I'm able to maneuver my way to the driver's side, catching a glimpse of the rest of the guys as they make their way to their vehicles. Some of the cameras follow them, but most stay on us.

"I'm going to need your keys," Justin holds his hand

out to Jordyn. Once she places them in his hands, he quickly shuts her door. He taps a couple times on the hood letting me know it's good to go.

Backing out slowly, because I don't put it past any one of these individuals to try anything to get us to stop, I get us out of the parking lot without any problems.

"That was intense," Jordyn looks behind her as we drive down the street.

Tapping her hand, I bring her attention back to me. "So what do you think of your first famous moment?"

"I was waiting for one of them to jump into the back of the truck."

"It's happened."

Her eyes go round and she looks behind her as though she's checking to make sure we don't have any unwanted passengers.

"This will only last for a little while. We always have to be aware that there may be a camera around, but this kind of mob only happens with big announcements or events," I go on to explain.

"Sorry about Justin."

"Why? He didn't do anything wrong. He was right, Scott should have been more prepared for this to happen after the announcement went live today. It doesn't take them long to figure out where everyone is, which leads me to a conversation I was wanting to have with you anyway."

"About what?"

"I was thinking about talking to Scott and bringing your brother on as one of our paid bodyguards."

Jordyn rolls her eyes and looks out her passenger window. This is the reason I wanted to speak to her first and not just bring it up to Scott. I want to know what her opinion is, how she would feel having her brother around a lot. She already makes comments about how he smothers her.

Brushing a couple fingers along her arm, I silently ask for her to look at me. When I have her eyes again, I continue, "Just hear me out. He is good at what he does, Jordyn, I saw that in just the short time it took for us to make it to the truck just now and I know he is worried about you. I know you want a little space, but I have to say I get what he is feeling. It won't be all of the time, but maybe it would put him at ease a little as well if he has a heads up on what's going on."

Jordyn takes a deep breath and moves her focus out the front windshield. I give her a moment to think about it without pushing her, if she says no, then that will be the end of it. It's just a suggestion on my part.

Giving her a couple minutes, I take her hand and squeeze it, her eyes are back to mine. "I get that you want to be independent and that you think you have this all under control. There are going to be days where it's just you and Megan and that mob of people is going to be there, wouldn't you feel better knowing you have your brother there? Hearing or not, Jordyn, those crowds can be ruthless."

It's in her eyes the moment she gives in and her head nods slightly in agreement.

"Does that mean yes?"

"As much as I hate to admit it, I felt a little calmer knowing he was there. On the other side of this, though, if he gets to be overprotective, I'm firing him."

Laughing, there it is, the brotherly-sisterly love. "Agreed."

"Can we get that pizza now? I'm starving."

A large pizza and two bottles of beer in front of us, I ask, "What type of movies do you like to watch?"

Shrugging, she grabs a slice of pizza.

"Come on, Jordyn, help a guy out. Action, girly, suspense? I know this isn't the ideal date, but judging by the crowd earlier, staying in tonight is probably the best plan, plus this way your brother won't be joining us."

Jordyn laughs, but it hasn't gone unnoticed that she seems a little withdrawn, plus she is just picking at the pizza, not really eating it.

"Hey, what's going on in that head of yours?"

Again, she shrugs.

"Jordyn, talk to me. Do you not like to watch movies?"

She rolls her eyes, "Who doesn't like to watch movies?"

"All right, do you just not want to watch one right now? You aren't saying something."

Jordyn takes a deep breath and I see it in her eyes when she gives in. "Fine, in my past experience with dating, I've found that not everyone likes to watch movies with a deaf person. If I'm watching a movie I have to have the subtitles on, that can bug a lot of people."

"Wait, you are telling me people have had a problem with that?" I ask in disbelief.

Who the hell were these guys that she's dated? Why would that be anything someone would complain about? I know it wasn't her family or friends, so that would mean she is talking about guys.

"Jordyn, I don't care if the words are large and in the middle of the screen."

Her face instantly changes. The worry I saw in her eyes is gone and there is a real smile on her face now. "I love action movies."

"I believe you just took another piece of my heart. Just for future reference, though, I'm not ashamed to say I like a good girly movie."

There is that smile that slams me in the chest every time I see it. "I'll keep that in mind."

Pizza box is empty, the movie is over and Jordyn is asleep in my arms. This feels perfect. Brushing a piece of hair away from her face, I think back to our earlier conversation about the subtitles with the movie. This woman is amazing. She is smart, compassionate, talented, independent, strong-minded, but her choice in previous guys is to be questioned.

How does any guy not just fall in love with this woman? I'm not really complaining, she's mine now and I'm not letting her go. She can watch a movie with subtitles, she can turn the radio up in the truck as loud as she wants to feel the beat, she is staying in my arms, however, it amazes me that men would be so shallow to believe their needs are more important than hers.

How does one not feel fortunate to just have this woman as their own? As strong and independent as she tries to put forward, I see that she easily backs down sometimes to make others more comfortable, especially when it's in regards to her being deaf. That's not the way it should be and I'm going to be more than happy to be the guy that shows that to her.

With a light touch, I brush my finger over her cheek, not wanting to startle her awake. It takes a moment but she begins to stretch and very slowly her eyes open. I watch her eyes as they look around the room as they focus and she tries to figure out where is she, but it doesn't take long for her eyes to meet mine.

"I'm so sorry. I didn't mean to fall asleep."

"Apology not needed, I'm not complaining."

Her eyes search mine and I want nothing more than to know what is going on in that head of hers. "Talk to me."

A small smile presses over her lips, her hand comes up and her fingers comb through my hair until they reach the back of my head. With light pressure she pulls my head down to her, our lips meeting.

This kiss starts out sweet, but it doesn't take long before she demands more and I'm more than willing to let her have control. Her tongue finds mine and before I know it, she is making her way onto my lap, straddling me. My arms now have the freedom to explore the body tightly pressed to mine. One arm wraps around her waist, my other hand gets lost in her hair, holding her tight to me.

Her hands slip in between us and I feel her fingers on the button of my shirt. Releasing my tight hold on her, my hands rest on her hips, giving her the ability to pull away slightly as she finishes the task she has started. Opening it up, her hands run over my chest and down my abs, making my stomach ripple at her touch.

Keeping my hands to myself is hard, but I'm enjoying her touches. She surprises me even more when her fingers leave my skin only to start the task of unbuttoning her own shirt. She doesn't remove her shirt, she lets it fall open and then she presses herself tightly against my chest.

Before taking my lips with her own, she says, "I love the way your skin feels against mine."

Those simple words are all it takes to send my need for her over the top and switch this around to me taking charge from this point. In one swift motion I'm up off the couch, her still in my arms, her legs wrapped tightly around my waist. This woman needs to be in my bed even if for only a little time tonight.

CHAPTER TWENTY-FIVE

JORDYN

I have no idea what has come over me, I think I have surprised myself just as much as I'm sure I have surprised Asher.

When he said that the captions across the movie were no big deal, it took a lot not to climb into his lap at that moment. Waking up in his arms and the look in his eyes when I was able to focus enough was all it took to reignite that need for him again.

As he carries me down the hallway toward where I'm assuming is his room, I keep my legs tightly wrapped around his waist which in turn is causing a friction that is driving me a little insane.

I feel his arm as it reaches for what I'm going to assume is the handle to his door. We go from the light hallway into the darkness. My legs unwrap from around him and I slide to the floor.

When he pushes the door shut behind us it leaves the room in almost complete darkness, I can make out his silhouette but not really anything else . His lips search out mine and his tongue instantly finds mine. There is a whole new excitement to this. No sound and very limited sight. I depend on my sight for everything, but this is something else. That flame igniting deep in my center is burning hotter at the anticipation of what's next.

Our first experience was outside in the daylight. I could see his eyes change colors, I could see his hands and know where they were going, his lips, his body's motions. Right now it's all touch and it's exciting.

Taking my hand, Asher leads me into the room, now that my eyes have adjusted a little I can make out the shape of the furniture but can't see the detail. After a moment, we stop.

"Asher, without the light I'm completely at your mercy. Normally I'd ask to turn them on, but the need this is causing to course through my veins is something I want to explore."

I can see the outline of his face, but no reactions. His lips crash against mine and I realize I don't need to see anything, just feel this man against me.

His hands make fast work of removing my already unbuttoned shirt and for a moment his hands roam, feeling all of my exposed skin.

Placing my hands on his chest, I work them up to his shoulders, pushing his shirt off as well. His hands leave my body to allow his shirt to fall from his arms, but quickly find me again.

My hands follow the warmth of skin from his chest to his abs, to the rougher material of his jeans, and without hesitation I unbuckle his belt, followed by the buttons of his jeans. His hands are working just as quickly on my remaining clothes.

With all of the urgency to rid each other of any and all barriers between us, he shifts gears suddenly as he gently lays be back on the bed, the softness taking over my body slightly cooling the heat radiating throughout me. When his lips lightly brush over one tight nipple I about explode off the bed, the heat coursing throughout my body like a bomb just went off.

Burying my fingers of one hand into the hair at the back of his head, I press him to me, silently begging him for more. My other hand that has a tight grip on his bicep feels the muscles flex, everything together is more than I can take.

Out at the lake we explored, right now all I want is him deep inside of me, nothing else is needed. My hand in his hair moves down his neck, over the tight muscles flexed in his back, to the lower back. My hand at his bicep moves to the hardness that my body is seeking.

"I need you, Asher." I'm hoping my words are loud enough for him to hear.

His lips move from my breast and crash against my lips. His arm circles around my waist and in one motion I feel myself scooted more onto the bed and him now joining me, his movement causing me to push my legs apart to accommodate him between them.

His lips never leaving mine, in one swift motion his enters me, my legs now coming up to wrap around his waist, my body silently begging for as much of him as I can take. His hips drive forward, mine thrusting up to meet his movement.

My very core pulsing as it begins to beg for more. Asher's movements become faster and I meet his every movement with my own need to have more. I feel my body starting to tighten around him. His lips leave mine and he buries his face into my neck. My hand on his back feels the vibrations, that's how I feel his sounds.

His movement becomes faster and faster and I match each one. I can feel myself tightening more and more and then before I can stop it to enjoy the motion of his body against mine longer, my release shoots through my body. His hips push once more into mine and his arms tighten around me as his body shivers with a slight vibration.

The room is still black and the only thing I feel is the rise and fall of Asher's chest under my cheek. Our legs are entwined, his arm holding me, my hand resting right above his heart. It's a rhythm I've found comfort and safety in, a beat that is starting to match my own.

This man has captured my heart so quickly. At times I still think that I'm going to wake up and find everything from the past week just a dream. There have been rehearsals, contracts signed, photoshoots, songs recorded, mobs of reporters and cameras everywhere. I've needed a bodyguard, hired a personal assistant, not to mention, tomorrow I'll be interviewed on T.V., and let's just top all of this off with this amazing guy now part of my life. I take in a deep breath and marvel at how fast everything has changed. Taking a deep breath, I take this moment to marvel over how lucky I am.

Asher moves under me, stretching his right arm out and before I can wonder too long on what he is doing, the light on the bedside table lights up the room. Adjusting my position slightly, I rest my chin on my hands that are now both resting on his chest.

"I can't talk to you in the dark," Asher smiles down at me. "That was a pretty deep breath you took there, everything all right?"

"If I ask you a question, will you answer it honestly?"

"That's a loaded question just as is, but sure."

"How many times have you talked to me and then realized I couldn't hear you?" I give him my best teasing smile.

Asher's cheeks actually start to turn a slight shade of red and for a moment I think he isn't going to answer my question, but nodding his head, he surprises me when he says, "All right, I'll admit, I've lost count."

I can't stop the laugh that bubbles up through my lips, he looks so cute when he is embarrassed.

Making my way up his chest, I claim his lips with my own. Yes, Asher James has stolen my heart and I'm completely his.

His fingers tangle in my hair and his other arm holds me tight to him. This is where I belong, there isn't a doubt in my mind.

Just his lips and the way his fingers tangle in my hair get that fire burning inside of me again, but before it can set ablaze, Asher ends the kiss.

"If there is any chance of me getting you home tonight, we need to go now. The longer we stay here in bed, the more likely I'm keeping you for the night."

"There is only one place I want to be tonight and it doesn't require us getting out of bed."

I don't miss the flicker of surprise in his eyes, "Are you sure?"

"We just need to leave early enough in the morning to stop by my place for a change of clothes. There is no way I'm going back tomorrow in the same clothes I wore today."

"We are men, we don't usually notice that kind of stuff."

"No, but Megan does."

Nodding his understanding, he says, "I'll agree to anything if I can keep you here with me tonight."

Asher tries to gracefully move from under me. "Just to let you know, I'm a pretty light sleeper, sneaking out of bed isn't going to work."

Slowly opening my eyes, I crane my neck back to look up at the man I just spent the night with. This felt right, waking up in his arms.

"I wasn't sneaking out of bed, my phone is going off in my pants on the floor. I've ignored it enough that the sound is getting louder and louder."

I smile, "I don't hear a thing."

HIs "yeah, whatever smile" turns to puzzlement and I can see that he wants to ask a question. "What's got that look on your face?"

"How do you wake up in the morning if you can't hear an alarm going off?"

"Like I said, I'm a light sleeper, so everything is connected to the light system in my apartment. The alarm is the lights flashing off and on. Some connect it to their bed so that it basically shakes them awake, but I prefer the lights."

"Well, my phone hasn't shut up and it's officially screaming at us to get up. If you want to stop by your place before we head over to the studio we better get up, plus I need breakfast."

"So what you are telling me is that I have to get out of bed."

Rolling us over and trapping me to the bed, he looks down at me, "I have no problem keeping you here in this bed, but you made me promise last night that I'd take you home before we went to the studio, something about not showing up in the same clothes."

His lips claim mine before I can respond. Who am I fooling? I would gladly take anything anyone said about my second-day-in-a-row attire and any looks I know I would get from Megan to stay right where I am.

Asher's lips leave mine to begin their trail down my neck, to one very tight nipple. Arching my back, I silently plead with him for more. My fingers bury in his hair, pressing him tightly to me.

My hips press up against his and I feel the vibration of his moan throughout my entire body. In one movement he gives me what I have been begging for, all of him, deep inside of me. His lips find mine once again and together we awaken our bodies. With each thrust of his hips I meet it with mine. It doesn't take long before I feel my body starting to tighten around him, starting to pull him in deeper and deeper. His face buries into my neck, my legs wrapping around his waist holding him tight to me as our bodies find our release together.

Waking up like this may be my new favorite.

179

CHAPTER TWENTY-SIX

ASHER

By the time we finally leave my house, we don't have time to make breakfast so we quickly grab breakfast burritos from one of my favorite little places and head straight to Jordyn's place so that she can grab a quick shower and change.

I offered her to take a shower with me, but she declined saying we would never get to the studio if we kept moving at the pace we were this morning. I personally enjoyed the pace, every movement of her body against mine.

Now she sits in the passenger seat, burrito in one hand, phone in the other. She is responding to text messages and her little giggles every once in a while start making me curious about who she is chatting with.

Tapping her arm, I get her attention. Nodding my head toward her phone, I ask, "Megan?"

"She wants to know where I am."

"She is at your apartment?"

Shaking her head no, she explains, "She stopped by thinking we would go to the studio together, but now she is just meeting me there."

Looking at her phone again, she then turns it to me showing me the time. "We are going to be late."

"I personally think we have a great excuse for being late."

"Asher, I don't want Scott thinking I'm not responsible."

"Relax, Jordyn, there will be plenty of time and Scott won't say a thing. It's a suggested time, we aren't going to be that far off if late at all."

Pulling up into a parking space at her complex, Jordyn jumps out of the truck before I even turn off the engine, burrito still in hand, eating as she runs up the stairs to her apartment. By the time I make it into the door, which she left wide open, I hear the water to the shower already running.

I sit on the couch to wait when my phone rings, it's a number I don't recognize, "Hello."

"Asher, this is Justin, Megan gave me your number. I've been trying to get ahold of Jordyn, Megan says she's with you."

"We are here at her place, she's in the shower right now, then we are heading over to the studio."

"All right, what studio? I'll meet you guys there."

Maybe talking to Scott about having him sign on isn't the best idea. I get being protective but he is going to have to give his sister a little breathing room.

"Honestly, Justin, I think everything will be all right

without the added security today. The studios are inside a guarded gate and..."

"I'm not worried about your security today, Asher, I have something I need to tell Jordyn and I think it's best if it's in person."

I now notice the change in Justin's voice, something is wrong. "Justin, what's going on?"

"I have security clearance already, I'll meet you guys there, which are you guys at today?"

After telling Justin which studio, he hangs up and an uneasy feeling settles in my chest. Something is wrong.

Couple of minutes later Jordyn comes out of her room, hair still wet, but dressed. Her phone is in her hand, "Hey, Justin has texted me a dozen times, but the final one says he will just talk to me when we get to the studio, any idea of what is going on? I've tried a couple texts back but he isn't responding."

"I just got off the phone with him, but he didn't say anything, just said he would see us at the studio."

"I didn't think we would need him today." Jordyn looks at me a little confused.

"All he told me is he needed to talk to you."

The ride to the studio is quiet. Jordyn just looks out the passenger window. When I reach over and take her hand, she holds mine, but never looks over at me.

Finally reaching the studio, we walk in and Scott meets us. He isn't his usual self and I don't have any time to ask him what's going on, there is a lady with him. "Jordyn, this is Kim, she will be doing makeup, just follow her and she will get you started."

"My brother is supposed to meet me here, have you seen him?"

"He is here somewhere, I'll have him meet you in your dressing room. Kim here has already been instructed about having to have eye contact when speaking to you. I'll have Megan join you when I see her."

Scott won't look at Jordyn when he speaks. His face is toward her, but his eyes stay down at a folder he is holding. Something is going on.

Jordyn looks as though she's going to say something, but Kim gets her attention and asks that she follow her. When Jordyn looks at me I se the concern in her eyes, but I smile and nod. "Go ahead, as soon as I find Justin I'll send him in your direction."

Nothing else is said, she just turns and follows Kim down the hallway.

"All right, Scott, what is going on?"

Scott takes a deep breath, I can see he is trying to control his emotions, but his eyes look glassed over. "Sean was found unresponsive by his daughter this morning at his home."

"What happened?"

"Asher, where is Jordyn?" Justin's voice comes from behind me.

"They just took her back to makeup. What's going on? Is Sean all right?"

I look to Justin but it's Scott that answers, "It's his heart. He called me about a month ago asking me again to listen to

Jordyn, that I wouldn't be sorry. He has spoken of Jordyn for a few years, but I was just getting started with you guys and Driven Roads, I had a full plate, that's when the idea came to me about adding a female voice to the group. He knows that the only dream Jordyn had was to be on stage and he knew that's where she belonged, but he knew no one would give her a chance if they knew she was deaf. That's when he also told me about his heart condition and how his heath was going down quickly. He had me promise not to speak of his health condition to anyone, especially Jordyn. I just got off the phone with his daughter. He isn't awake but he is stable. They are just trying to make him comfortable."

"The other day when he stopped by he didn't look well," I remember thinking he looked real tired.

"Why did he go to your house?" Justin asks from behind me.

I couldn't help the small smile, "He was playing the fatherly role and making sure my intentions with Jordyn were pure."

"When Jordyn finds out, she is going to want to go to him right away," Megan walks over to us now.

"That's were my dilemma is. Sean called me the other day, I think he knew, but he made me promise to not let her walk away from any of the scheduled plans if something was to happen. He is so proud of her and excited that her dreams are coming true." Scott looks to Justin for some kind of answers.

"Mr. Emly has been a very large part of Jordyn's life for a long time now. She won't forgive any of us if we don't tell her what is going on and allow her to be the one to make the call on what is best for her to do. He may be stable right now, but if something happens in the next couple of hours before she knows, she isn't going to forgive any of us." Megan gives Justin the look, basically saying he knows she is right.

"It's not right for any of us to make the decision for her," I answer for everyone, "plus, none of us would forgive ourselves if something happened and we kept this quiet. I understand why Sean asked Scott to do what he did, but she is already going to be upset that his health was kept from her, let alone this."

"We can't all walk in there to tell her." Justin doesn't look extremely excited to be the one to break the news to his sister.

"I'll go and tell her." I turn and head down the hall before anyone says anything else.

Walking into the door I watched Jordyn and Kim disappear into just a few minutes ago, I find Jordyn already sitting in the chair in front of a large mirror and Kim is already starting to apply her makeup.

Jordyn's eyes connect with mine through the mirror. "Asher, have you seen Justin yet?"

"Kim, do you mind if we have a moment, please?"

"Absolutely." Kim must have seen something in my eyes because she quickly leaves us alone in the room.

"Asher, I'm really starting to panic now, what's going on?" Jordyn turns in her chair to look at me.

There is no easy way to tell her. "This morning Scott and your parents received a call from Sean's daughter. She found him unresponsive at his home. He is at the hospital now, they are making him comfortable, but it is basically just time now."

Tears instantly brighten Jordyn's eyes and she is fighting very hard to not allow them to fall as she tries to take in the news. I close the space between us, but don't take her into my arms just yet. I see that she is trying to compose herself and I want her to know I'm here if she needs my shoulder to cry on or the strength she needs to decide what she needs to do. I can see the struggle throughout all of her features as she looks around the room, fighting with herself.

"I need to speak to his daughter." Jordyn's voice is just above a whisper.

Holding a finger up to signal her to wait, I open the door and look back down the hallway where Scott, Justin and Megan as still standing. "Who has his daughter's number?"

Justin holds up his phone first, "Mom and Dad texted it to me."

"Jordyn wants to speak to her, maybe you should be in here just to ensure communication."

Justin nods and makes his way toward me. "How is she?" he asks before he comes into the room.

"Your sister is a very strong woman."

"Yeh, sometimes she acts too strong." Justin walks past me into the room.

Jordyn is still sitting in her chair, "I need to speak to his daughter."

Justin looks down at his phone and starts tapping on the screen. "I just messaged her and let her know who this number belongs to and that we'll be video calling."

Moments later, a lady appears on his screen who looks to be in her mid-thirties. "Hello, I'm Justin, Jordyn's brother, she would like to talk to you. I'm sure you know she is deaf, but as long as she can see your lips she can hold a pretty good conversation with you, although I'm here to sign to her if she doesn't understand something."

"My father speaks of Jordyn a lot, I understand and am glad you guys have called. I'm here at the hospital with him now."

Justin hands his phone over to Jordyn. She takes a couple deep breaths and then brings the screen up to her face.

"Jordyn, I'm happy to finally meet you, Dad talks about you all of the time. I'm Leah, his oldest daughter."

CHAPTER TWENTY-SEVEN

JORDYN

My heart is tearing apart and I'm doing everything I can to hold back the tears. My first instinct is to leave and go straight to the hospital, but something is keeping me here. Mr. Emly only wanted one thing for me and that was for my dream of performing to come true. He knew how much it meant for me to be on stage, singing. This interview today is part of the experience, part of my dreams coming true.

"It's nice to meet you, Leah, I wish it was over a happier conversation. What is happening, what are the doctors saying?"

I watch as her lips move, but it's hard to focus on what she is saying. It's his heart, and it's been something he has been dealing with for a very long time. As each word that is formed passes her lips, I feel the strength that I'm trying so hard to keep melting away. From the background I can tell she is in the room with him, her final words are what strike the deepest. "The doctors say it's just a matter of time now, he is done fighting."

My mind flashes back to the first day we met Mr. Emly. I was trying not to be excited because I knew my chances of ever fulfilling my childhood dreams of performing were pretty much lost the moment that car hit us, or at least that is what I kept telling myself. Mr. Emly, on the other hand, never doubted I could do it. From the first moment he signed hello and introduced himself in sign language, a new hope filled me and an amazing man become part of my life. He has given me the greatest gift, he gave me Driven Roads.

Justin touches my shoulder, bringing my attention back to what's happening today. "Jordyn, are you understanding everything Leah is telling you?" he signs.

I know Mr. Emly wouldn't want me to miss today's opportunity, but I need to speak to him once more.

Looking from my brother back to the screen I'm holding in my hand, I say, "I need to say something to him, can you please put the phone by him?"

Leah nods and I watch the screen as Leah moves it around the room and when the image stops, I can see Mr. Emly lying on the bed. I almost drop the phone at the sight I wasn't as prepared for as I thought. The man who was like another father to me, lying in a hospital bed.

Asher is next to me and holding my free hand, being the strength I need to say what I want Mr. Emly to hear.

"Mr. Emly, the strength I have right now to fulfill what I know you would want me to do is what you taught me to have. This gift you've handed me is holding me here when I want nothing more than to be there with you, but I know that isn't where you would want me. I do need to say thank you. Thank you for everything you have given me. You not only gave me the tools to continue on with my passion, but the strength to believe in myself as well. Every beat of the music that I feel will remind me of you and the amazing gift you have given me. Thank you for giving a scared deaf girl a chance. I love you and am honored that I'll always have a piece of your passion for music in me. I promise to never let you down and make the most out of something we both love, the beat and vibration of the song."

My body is shaking and I can no longer hold the phone, it's taken from my hands and just as the tears begin to fall, I find myself in Asher arms.

I'm not sure how long Asher has been standing here just holding me, but I do know I have to pull myself together to get through this interview. Pulling myself from the warmth of Asher's chest is hard, I just want to curl up and have him hold me while I cry some more.

Sitting up, I begin to wipe the tears away from my face and look for a tissue for my nose. Asher reads my mind when he reaches behind him and grabs one off of the makeup counter.

"Are you sure you want to go through with this? No one would blame you if you decided not to appear today."

"Mr. Emly would. I need to do this for him." Taking a couple of deep breaths, I try to settle the shaking in my hands.

Asher grabs my hands and brings them up to his lips, kissing my knuckles, "I'm going to be right beside you the whole time. If you are losing the strength, reach out to me and I'll be the strength you need to make it through it, all right?"

"You know, Mr. Emly has given me so much more than just a band to sing in, he brought you into my life as well."

Leaning forward, he lightly kisses me, pulling back just enough for me to see his face and lips. "A gift I will forever cherish."

Before anything else can be said, the door opens and Megan pokes her head in. "I don't mean to interrupt but they are wondering if you are good to go with makeup?"

Asher kisses me on the forehead, "If you need me, send Megan to come get me."

Asher leaves the room, Justin following him out and Megan walks over, wrapping me up in a hug. I give her a moment, but I know if I allow her to hug me much longer I'm going to lose my fight with the tears again.

Pulling out of Megan's hug, I turn myself to the mirror again. "Let Kim know I'm ready."

Megan wants to say something, but I'm thankful when she decides against it and walks to the door. Moments later, Kim walks in.

"I'm sorry for the puffy eyes." I know my apologetic smile is full of sadness but I try anyway.

"Don't worry about it at all, it's my job to make those disappear."

This is the largest daytime talk show on television and as I sit back here and watch the production crew instruct the live audience and set up the stage, my nerves begin to build. They wanted me to wait in my dressing room, but I needed to get out and walk around. Megan hasn't left my side and has been the one chatting with everyone who stops to ask questions or give direction. I still feel like I'm in a fog.

A strong arm drapes across my shoulders, I didn't even see my brother walk up to me. "Hey, are you all right?"

Nope, there isn't a feeling in me that I would describe as all right, is what I want to tell him but instead I smile, "I'm fine, have you heard anything else from Leah?"

He shakes his head, "No, she did tell me she would call or text if anything changed."

A gentleman walks up to us and introduces himself as the producer, "We have about thirty minutes before air time. I'd like to have you join the rest of the group in the standby room at this time, please."

"No problem, thank you."

"Come on, I'll go with you," Justin, with his arm still draped over my shoulder, turns me and leads me in the direction given by the man.

The large television in the room is live feeding the show as it starts. Today seems like a dream. The amount of emotions I've experienced has left me exhausted, all I can say is thank goodness for makeup.

As we are directed to backstage and the introduction of the band is being made, a sudden calmness washes over me. Looking over my shoulder, I find my brother and see that he is looking at his phone. Something tells me I know what he is looking at. Justin looks up from his phone and nods, his eyes are sad and I know, Mr. Emly is gone. I take Asher's hand and a couple of deep breaths. He looks down at me, his eyes questioning me if I'm all right.

Nodding, I give him a small smile and am happy when he continues to hold my hand as we are introduced out onto stage and together we walk out. Looking around, I can see all of the clapping and excitement, I really wish I could hear it, though.

Waving and smiling, I'm hoping no one can tell my world has just been flipped upside down. Asher leads me to the couch where I sit between him and Noah. The other four guys take the high chairs behind the couch. Megan takes her spot over by the host as the interrupter.

We weren't going to have Megan join us on stage, I don't want to hide anything but I don't want all the attention to be on the fact that I'm deaf for the whole interview. I was pretty sure of my abilities to understand everything, but with the day's events we decided it was best to have her join us.

We sit and wave, the show's producers allows the time for the cheering of the audience, but they all quiet down with the signal from the staff.

"Hello, guys," the host starts the show off, "it's been what, a year since you have been here?"

"Yes, right after we released our second album," Asher speaks for the group.

"Well, it looks like the group has grown a little since then," the host points over at me.

"Yes, we are here to introduce our newest member of

Driven Roads, Jordyn Collins, our female vocalist," Asher continues to answer the for the group.

"Yes, we have all seen your new member and what I know everyone is eager to learn about is the new relationship between the two of you." The host waves a hand between Asher and myself.

"They don't hide that part very well," Noah pipes in before Asher can say anything, causing the audience to laugh.

I have to admit, I'm glad we decided to bring Megan out with us, everything is happening so fast and without being able to see everyone, I'm able to keep up with her signing for me.

"We'll get to the romance part in a minute. First, what made you guys decide to add a member to the group? You guys have been hitting the top of the charts, it's not like you needed the extra push."

"Actually, it was suggested by our agent, but when we all heard her sing, we knew she was the perfect fit for the group," Zayden is the first to answer the question.

I can't help the smile that spreads across my face, and when I look behind me at him, he gives me a wink. I know how Asher feels, but I can't say I haven't wondered if the band feels the same way or they were just going along for the ride. They've never made me feel unwelcome, but it's nice to know they agree with having me around.

"I know everyone is curious, it's hard to ignore the woman sitting here to my left signing and not ask questions. Jordyn, is there a hearing loss?"

"Actually, I'm deaf."

"Wait, you mean you hear nothing at all?"

"Yes, I have complete loss of hearing. I lost my hearing at the age of ten in a car accident."

"So how do you sing if you can't hear the music?"

"I feel the music. The vibration on the floor, the beat in my chest." Taking a deep breath, I continue, "I had an amazing teacher, Mr. Emly, who took on the challenge of teaching a deaf child to feel the music. My passion has always been to sing, he made sure I had all the abilities to fulfill that dream."

Asher's hand squeezes mine, and I'm holding it together, that is until Noah takes my other hand in his and then I feel the hands of the guys behind me on my shoulders. I take a deep breath and will the tears in my eyes to disappear.

"This Mr. Emly, he seems pretty remarkable."

"Without him, I wouldn't have this."

CHAPTER TWENTY-EIGHT

ASHER

It doesn't surprise me that Jordyn falls asleep within moments of us getting into the truck. I've texted Megan and asked her to run by Jordyn's place and pick a few things up so that we don't have to stop by there in the morning before the radio interview and performance we have scheduled for tomorrow.

She meets me at the diner I'm ordering our dinner from.

"How is she doing?" I see the concern in Megan's eyes.

"She fell asleep the moment we pulled out of the studio's lot. I just figure it's best that she isn't alone tonight."

"Trust me, she wouldn't have been alone, but I'm glad she is with you. I'm glad she has finally found someone who will put her first and not make her feel like she has to figure out how to fit into their world."

"What man wouldn't want to be in her world?"

Shrugging, Megan looks into the truck at her best

friend still sleeping in the passenger seat. "She has only dated a couple of guys and none of them are worth talking about, trust me. She is going to try and act strong through all of this, she needs the shoulder to lean on, Mr. Emly was very special to her."

"I know and she is stubborn and tries to be very independent. I've got her, I promise. Did she tell you we are hiring on her brother?"

Megan's eyes fly open in surprise, "No, when did all of this happen?"

"Actually, we just talked about it. He'll basically be around with you two more than anything."

"If Jordyn is good with it so am I." Megan hands me Jordyn's bag, "Tell her if she needs me I'm only a text or video chat away. If anything, I'll see you two at the studio tomorrow. Hopefully with how busy you guys are the next couple of weeks, it'll kind of keep her mind too busy to think of everything that happened today."

Opening the door to the backseat of my truck, I placed the bag Megan handed me on the seat. "I'm going to run in and pick up our dinner."

"See you guys tomorrow."

I watch as Megan gets back into her car and wait until she pulls out of the parking lot before I make my way into the diner to pick up our dinner.

Once at home, I grab everything and run it into the house before coming back outside and getting Jordyn from the truck. Opening the door she jumps, looking around and trying to get her bearings about where she is.

Placing a hand on her leg, I wait for her eyes to find mine. "Sorry, I didn't mean to scare you."

"No, I'm sorry," she rubs her hands over her eyes, "I didn't mean to fall asleep. We're back at your house?"

"I didn't think you should be alone tonight. I had Megan grab some of your things and I grabbed us dinner on the way home."

I know she stayed with me last night, but maybe I shouldn't have assumed she would be all right with staying here tonight as well. I didn't want her to be alone.

"If you would rather I take you home, we can eat dinner and then I can drive you over."

I step back, giving her some room as she steps down out of the truck. Once her feet touch the ground, she closes the space between us and gives me a gentle kiss.

"I don't want to be alone tonight, and wouldn't want to be any other place than here with you. Thank you for thinking of everything."

Relief washes through me. "Hungry?"

"A little, yes."

Grabbing her hand, I lead her up to the house.

After dinner, I try to convince Jordyn to go and relax in a bath, but she only wants a shower and then asks if I will just sit and watch a movie with her. We pick a comedy but within twenty minutes she is fast asleep in my arms.

Today during the interview, I was impressed with how composed she stayed, especially during the time she was talking about Sean.

Listening to her telling Sean goodbye over the phone was heart breaking, but the strength she possessed throughout the call was amazing. I know she wanted nothing more than to go to the hospital to be with him, but again, she thought of someone else's needs or feelings over hers. She knew Sean wouldn't want her to miss today, she stayed for him and what he would have wanted for her.

Turning off the television, I'm tempted to just throw the blanket from the back of the couch over the two of us and sleep here for the night. I don't want to wake her and I know the moment I move she is going to wake up, but the idea of my comfortable bed just down the hall wins out.

Placing a hand under her head that is resting in my lap, I gently raise it to make my way off the couch so that I can pick her up.

"I'm awake, like I said, light sleeper."

Her eyes were still closed so responding would have meant I was talking to myself, instead I pick her up into my arms and make the way down the hall.

"I can walk, Asher."

Looking down at her, her eyes are half open now and she is looking up at me.

"I'm aware that you can walk, but I like having you in my arms."

Laying her down on the bed, I tuck the blankets around her and make my way to the bathroom to grab a quick shower.

She is still cuddled deep into the comforter when I join her in bed. She adjusts herself so that she is lying on her side looking straight at me.

"What's going through that head of yours?" I ask.

Jordyn smiles, her hand comes up and she brushes it down the side of my face, her eyes are searching mine. She wants to say something, but she is holding back.

"Jordyn, talk to me. I see it in your eyes. If you want to talk about Sean, I'm here to listen."

Her eyes instantly glass over at the mention of Sean's name. I have to fight the urge to take her into my arms and just hold her, but there is something there that is holding me back.

Her eyes close and she takes a couple of deep breaths. One tear escapes, with a light finger I wipe it away. At my touch, her eyes open again.

"You've been so strong today. From the moment you talked to Sean on the phone, to the interview today, and even now. I'm here, Jordyn, you can use my shoulder, chest, whatever to cry on, it's not showing weakness."

She smiles, "It's been a week. That's it. My life has gone from this quiet world to a visual fast pace race. Mr. Emly told me one day I would have my dreams on the stage, that the world would be missing a beautiful gift if I was kept quiet. I'd roll my eyes at him every time he told me this," she laughs slightly, but the sound is cut off when the tears flow a little more.

I have to fist my hands to keep them from reaching out. She isn't done, there is more that she wants to say. The comfort she needs right now is for me to listen.

"He has given me this gift, Driven Roads, and with it, you. I have been so tied up with all of this that I didn't see the signs that something was going on. The short text messages, the fact that he hasn't been around at all. I should have gone over to his house, I should have stopped for just a moment during this insane week and realized something wasn't right."

"Jordyn, stop. The last thing Sean would want right

now is you beating yourself up for something you had no control over."

"Maybe I should have left the interview today and went to the hospital."

"Sean stood back and gave you just enough response this past week to keep your head where he knew it needed to be. He heard you today, Jordyn. Being at the hospital wouldn't have changed anything, you were exactly where he wanted you to be and I know you know that."

"How am I supposed to do this now, without him around, if for nothing else but to be that support?"

"By doing exactly what you told him today on the phone that you would. Always feeling the beat of the song, by teaching the hearing world, like you have taught me, that there is so much more to a song than what you can hear. Show the world what Sean has taught you."

CHAPTER TWENTY-NINE

JORDYN

The morning light shining throughout the room is what wakes me up this morning. I'm surprised when I roll over to find myself alone in Asher's large bed. Looking around, I've no idea what time it is, and I've no idea where I left my phone.

My head is pounding this morning, I'm sure from the emotional rollercoaster yesterday, but there isn't much in me at the moment that wants to get out of bed. I'd like nothing more than to stay in the warmth of this bed, buried under all of the covers, having nothing to do with the outside world and the fact that Mr. Emly is no longer here. If I could hide here I could pretend yesterday didn't happen.

We have the radio interview this afternoon. I need to go on with this day like nothing is wrong. Throwing the large blankets over my head, I sink into the darkness it provides. I think this is the hardest part of all of this famous stuff. Even when your day is going downhill, you have to put a smile on your face and act as though every-thing is great.

The mattress dips down and the covers are lifted gently, revealing the light of the room and it causes me to squint as my eyes adjust to the light.

"Can I just stay here, in bed, all day?"

Looking up at Asher, he gives me an understanding smile, "I'd have no problem at all lying in bed with you all day, but we have to be at the studio in two hours."

"Two hours... What time is it?"

"It's a little after eleven. I was letting you sleep as long as I could, but we do have to get moving."

"Eleven, why didn't you wake me up earlier?"

"You needed to sleep. I figured when I got up and you didn't even flinch when I moved you, or when I came in twice to check on you and you hadn't moved from where I left you, you needed the sleep."

"Not going to lie, not much of me that wants to move now."

Asher pushes a piece of hair away from my face, leans over and gives me a sweet kiss. Standing up, he reaches a hand out to me, "Come on."

"Fine," grabbing his hand, I make my way out of the comfort of the bed and onto my feet.

Asher wraps his arms around me holding me tight to him. Burying my face against his chest, we stand this way for a while. Nothing needs to be said, this is the comfort I need.

Taking a deep breath, I need to pull myself together, today's plans aren't going to change because my world was flipped upside down yesterday.

Slightly pushing back, Asher releases his hold, when he looks down at me I see the slight worry in his eyes.

"I'm all right," I reassure him. "We need to get moving, I don't want to be late."

"I thought we would stop and grab some lunch before heading over to the studio."

I step out of his arms, "All right, let me grab a fast shower and get ready real quick, I won't be long."

Before I can step away, Asher's arms are circling me again. "Jordyn, I'm here if you need to talk. This isn't easy and the outer appearance strength you are determined to show is going to be exhausting. I'm here to lean on."

"Thank you." I stretch up slightly on my toes and kiss him, "I promise I'm all right. Now let me go and get ready, or you aren't going to get lunch first."

Pulling out of his arms is hard. I want nothing more than to have him hold me, but our day needs to begin.

Pulling up to the building home to the radio station, we are greeted with an instant mob of flashes and people. Before I even have a chance to think about how I'm getting out of the truck and to the entrance, my door is opened and my brother is by my side.

"You know, you are more work than most of the pop stars I've been hired to protect, difference is this isn't crazy fans, it's insane media. You two created quite a stir with that first kiss picture. Wasn't enough to just join the band," his hands are moving with his mouth.

"Just remember, you wanted to be overprotective," I remind him.

His expression changes from kidding to a more serious one, "Are you up for this today?"

I know it's a small smile, but I smile. "I'm good," I reassure him.

Justin looks over to Asher, as if asking for reassurance.

"Hey," I speak first before Asher can say anything. Justin looks back at me, "Trust me, I'm all right."

Justin searches my face for a moment, but nods and moves back to allow me room to get out of the truck. Together we walk to the front of the truck where Asher is now waiting. Asher takes my hand and together we push through the mob, following behind my brother and one other of the group's bodyguards.

Scott meets us at the door, yesterday has affected him as well. They were good friends, I believe if anyone here understands my feelings today it's him.

"Everyone else is back in the studio, we are on in thirty." Scott's eyes and energy level aren't the same today as they usually are, but he is in manager mode, probably pushing through the same as I am.

"Oh, um, Scott, I gave Megan the day off, she has some business to finish up with her previous job and I didn't really feel the need to have her here today. She wants to get everything with them settled before we leave next week."

"She has already sent me a text, it's all good. I'm a little concerned about how you are going to do with understanding the questions from the host, mics will be in front of your faces," he turns and starts heading down the hall to the studio.

Turning around, Justin is still standing between Asher

and myself, and the door leading outside. "Do you mind coming in with me?" I signed.

"My job description keeps getting longer and longer," he gives me a teasing smile as he signs his response.

"Good thing you love the person you are working for."

Justin loops an arm around my shoulders, "Come on, Scott is yelling at us from down the hall."

The interview isn't much different from the show yesterday. They play our new song, we take calls from fans, nice thing about being on the radio, the atmosphere is a lot more laid back. No hair and makeup beforehand, no audience to entertain, we could yawn and no one saw it. I much prefer this type of interview over the in-person ones.

Asher's hand takes mine as we pull out of the studio's parking lot. Bringing my attention from the passenger window of the truck, I look at him.

"So what did you think of today's interview?"

"A lot more laid back, it was kind of nice."

"Yep, I prefer radio over television any day. I have a couple errands to run today, are you wanting to come with me?"

"Actually, if you don't mind just taking me home, I'm needing a little time."

Megan was busy working all day, and with Asher having some stuff to go and do, it would be the perfect opportunity to sit and be alone for a little while, something I haven't had much of the past week.

We stop at a red light and Asher looks over at me, a worried look in his eyes.

"Stop looking at me like that. I'm fine. Yes, I'm still upset and all but I really haven't had any time to think and process. I'd like a little time to myself. It takes a lot to move throughout the day when you can't hear anything. I work harder on making sure I don't miss anything, to catch the conversations, I constantly have my head on a swivel. I know this sounds completely contradicting but I need the quiet."

Taking my hand in his, Asher kisses my knuckles. He understands.

"Light's green," I smile at him, tipping my head in the direction of the windshield.

Pulling up into a parking space, Asher jumps out of the driver's seat and quickly rounds the truck to the passenger side before I even have a chance to open the door. It doesn't go unnoticed, though, that his eyes are everywhere but on me.

Hopping down, I ask, "Hey, what's wrong?"

"I really don't like that this place has no gate, it's just a matter of time before the vultures with the cameras find out where you live."

Reaching up, I wind my arm around his neck and bring his eyes and mouth to me. Asher's arms instantly circle my waist and bring me tight against him. His tongue finds mine, and I'm pushed up against the passenger seat of the truck.

As quickly as the kiss starts, Asher ends it. "If I don't leave now, I won't be leaving at all."

As tempting as it is, I do need this time alone.

"Come on, I'll walk you up to your apartment."

"It's all right, I'm good." If he walks me up, I'm going to have a harder time saying goodbye at the door. He has things to do and I need a little time to process everything.

"Are you sure?"

"Yes."

"All right, I'm going to text after I finish some errands, we have nothing on the schedule for tomorrow, so maybe we can take a little trip back to the lake. A little time for you and me, no cameras, no interviews, no band."

"Sounds like a great idea." Pushing up on my toes, I take one last quick kiss, "I'll talk to you later."

CHAPTER THIRTY

ASHER

I watch as Jordyn walks up the stairs to her apartment. From this spot, I can see her door. I wait until she is inside before I round the truck, back to the driver's side. My eyes are on a constant swivel watching for any signs that someone followed us from the studio. It's only a matter of time before they find out where she lives.

Hopping up into the seat, I pull out my phone and find Justin's number.

It rings twice before he answers, "Everything all right?"

"What if I just wanted to call and say hi?"

"Asher, man, I know you are dating my sister and all, and the last couple of days we have seen a lot of each other, but honestly, not expecting the 'just called to say hi' call yet."

I know once Justin and I have a little more time to get to know each other, we are going to get along great.

"Agreed, but you need to calm down a little, man, she is already worried you are going to smother her, don't assume every time one of us calls it's a bad thing. Which, not going to lie, is totally contradicting on the reason for this call."

"Not a way to make a man feel better." His worried voice returns again.

"Nothing like that. I'm actually sitting in the parking lot of her apartment right now. She is safe and in her place, but I'm going to need your help convincing her she may have to find another place to live."

"Asher, if this is your way of asking me how I feel about her moving in with you, way too soon, man."

Not that I'll admit it to him, but the thought has crossed my mind. "Look, I'm crazy about your sister, but that may be rushing things just a little."

I hear Justin's deep sigh of relief on the other end of the phone and smile to myself.

"Look, this place has no gate around it, all it's going to take is one person to follow us and this place is going to be public knowledge. She is laughing the situation off, but you and I both know what can happen."

"I agree with you completely, but like you said earlier, I can't be the one to convince her, she'll think I'm just being overprotective. The person you need to talk to is Megan, she'll have a better chance of getting her to listen."

He's right, that may be the only person she even begins to listen to. "I'll give Megan a call. Before I go, again, I said not to smother her too much, but someone might want to check on her tonight. She is trying so hard to be strong but I see it in her eyes, losing Sean is killing her. I told her I would check in later, but you may want to have maybe one of your parents check in or something."

"Will do."

"All right, talk to you later," hanging up the phone, I glance around one last time.

It takes everything in me not to go up and just tell her I'm staying with her tonight, but then I realize I'm starting to sound like Justin. She is a grown woman and can take care of herself. She needs time right now and I'm going to give it to her. However, I'm going to text Megan and see if I can get her on my side about convincing Jordyn it's time to find a new place to live.

After running a few errands, I text Jordyn and ask how she is doing. She replies back with a brief text stating that she is lying in the bath tub, reading a book, and relaxing. Noah had texted earlier asking if I wanted to meet up with him and a couple of the guys for a beer. It would keep me from being home, wishing I was with Jordyn so I'm now on my way to meet up with the guys.

Walking in I spot Noah, Jesse and Dean sitting over at a round pub table.

"Hey, look who is joining us," Jesse greets me as I walk up to the table.

"And is alone," Dean adds.

"You know, I can't even give you a hard time and say the girl doesn't let you go out and play alone because Jordyn is too cool for that. It's more like you finally let her out of your sight." Jesse smacks me on my back.

A waitress comes by, "Can I get you something?"

"A beer, please."

She looks around at the guys, "Anything for you guys?"

Noah holds his mug up, "No thanks, we are good."

She stands at our table for a moment and looks at each of us in turn. Her smile begins to grow along with her eyes.

"We are here for a couple of beers and some downtime," Noah uses his smooth voice and country boy charm on the waitress the moment she realizes who she is waiting on.

Her head bobs up and down as though she understands what he is saying to her in code, and she turns with a huge smile on her face. We all watch as she walks away, looking over her shoulder a couple of times to make sure we don't disappear.

"So, speaking of Jordyn, how is she doing?" Dean takes a drink of his beer.

"Right now, she is taking a little time to herself at home. She is trying to be so strong in front of everyone, pushing through these interviews."

"This weekend isn't real crazy, well, except my little girl's birthday party that you all better be coming to, but after that it's all go until after the festival next weekend." Jesse reminds us of our upcoming schedule.

The waitress comes back and places my beer on the table. "Our policy is to not bother anyone famous when they come in, and I promise to be professional, but I have to ask, even if it means the risk of getting fired," she places her notepad that she was using to take orders down on the table in front of me, "can I please get your autographs?"

Her wide eyes beg each of us in turn around the table. Then she looks over her shoulder to see if anyone is watching her.

We each sign the notebook and hand it back to her, she doesn't say anything after that, just walks away.

"I'm not going to lie, this part is never going to get old." Noah sits back in his chair and smiles.

Shaking his head at Noah, Dean turns his attention on me, "So, from what I'm seeing, things with Jordyn are getting serious pretty fast. She is great, don't get me wrong on that, but what is so special to make it so fast?"

Dean and I have known each other since we were in the second grade. We are more like brothers than friends.

"It's not all about her." I take a drink of my beer. "What I mean is she doesn't want the world to revolve just around her. She doesn't need special treatment, she wants to make things easier for everyone else and adapt to a world she can no longer hear in, and all I want to do is learn her world. She had her sounds taken from her, and I can never image how that was for her, but what Sean taught her and how she feels the music is amazing. It gives a person a whole new appreciation for the sounds put together to make our songs. It was her voice, though, that reeled me in. So pure, so much heart, her being beautiful, kind-hearted and grounded was just what topped it all off."

"Great, he is starting to talk like Jesse did when he met Kaitlyn." Noah rolls his eyes and then dodges the wadded napkin that Jesse throws at him.

"Man, I would watch what you say, this isn't something you plan, it just hits you like a ton of bricks," I explain.

I can't wait for the day Noah finds his match in a woman. I'd say out of all of us, my little brother is the playboy of the group. Being the youngest, I'm sure it's going to take him a little longer to think about settling down.

Our waitress arrives back at the table with a beer for each of us, and my point is proven as she turns to walk away and Noah's eyes follow her.

"So you are saying Jordyn is it for you?" Dean asks.

"All I'm saying is it's off to a great start."

"I'll admit when Scott suggested to us that he thought it was a good idea to add a female voice to the group, I thought he was insane. We are doing great as a guy band. After witnessing the two of you singing together and seeing what that connection between you adds to the song, that's what country music is made of. The fans are going to go nuts." Jesse toast his beer in the air before taking a drink.

Noah stands up and moves to my side, draping his arm over my shoulders, "It's killing you right now to be here and not with her, isn't it?"

Shrugging his arm off my shoulders and pushing him back to his seat, I assure him, "I'm only worried because of the events of yesterday."

The mention of yesterday and Sean's passing takes the playful smile off my brother's face. "I'm sorry, I'll lay off a little."

Pulling out my phone, I shoot Jordyn a quick text.

Me: Just want to say goodnight. I'll text in the morning

and maybe we can plan something if you are feeling up to it.

It doesn't take long for Jordyn to text back.

Jordyn: Everything is good. Goodnight. Talk to you tomorrow.

CHAPTER THIRTY-ONE

JORDYN

I had fallen asleep with my phone next to me in bed last night, so when it vibrated next to me for the fifth time, I could no longer ignore it.

Rubbing my eyes, I try to adjust to the sunlight shining through my bedroom window. Picking up my phone, I see Megan's face icon on the screen with the number five next to it. It's only seven, seriously, our day to relax and she couldn't wait maybe two more hours to blow up my phone?

Swiping the screen, my phone opens right up to her text message.

Megan: Have you seen the new picture?

Megan: You need to wake up.

Megan: JORDYN

Really, all in caps, like that was going to wake me up. Before I continue to read her remaining text messages, I open up the web browser of my phone. Top news box, there it is, a picture of Asher and I kissing by his truck yesterday when he dropped me off.

Headline: This is how country music is created.

Right under the image: If there were any doubters about this hot romance blooming between Asher James and new band member Jordyn Collins just being for publicity, this picture of the two will definitely prove the fire between the them. You can't fake that kind of heat.

Letting my phone drop to the pillow next to me, I cross my arms over my eyes. It's way too early for all of this. I feel my stomach rumble and realize I didn't eat anything for dinner last night. I'd decided to relax in a bubble bath and got into a new book that I'd started reading. Once my body turned to a prune and the water was cold, I moved from the bathtub to my bed. Right now, I don't want to think about the new image of Asher and I floating over social media, I just want some food.

Grabbing my phone and ignoring the last two text messages from Megan, I text her back.

Me: Want to meet up for breakfast? I'm starving now that you have woken me up.

Stretching, I wait for her response, which takes all of two seconds.

Megan: Really, are we just going to not talk about what's flying around the internet right now?

Me: I'm hungry, want to meet me at the diner for breakfast?

Megan: Fine. I'll meet you, and then we talk. That picture is hot.

Rolling my eyes, I shoot a text back saying I'll meet her

in an hour. Placing my phone on the nightstand, I roll out of bed and head to the bathroom for a shower, hoping it will help to wake me up a little.

As I'm getting dressed, the screen lighting up on my phone catches the corner of my eye, but I ignore it, assuming it's my alerts going off from my news feed or social media.

Once I'm ready, I grab my phone off the nightstand and head for the front door. As I'm walking down the stairs ,my phone vibrates in my hand. Looking down, it's a message from Justin.

Rolling my eyes, I'm pretty sure it's safe to assume he has seen the picture this morning and is calling to play the big brother role and lecture me. Ignoring it, I shove my phone into my back pocket.

Rounding to the driver's side of my Jeep and clicking the unlock button, I go to open the door and flashes of light start bouncing off my driver's door window. What the...

That's when I see in the reflection in the window of a mob of people, all with cameras, surrounding me and my Jeep.

Turning to face half of the mob, my back firmly pressed against the door of my Jeep, I have cameras flashing in my face, microphones being shoved at me and I have not a clue what any of them are saying.

Putting up my hands, I try to talk over them and ask them to move back, but they act as though I'm not saying a word and they are starting to close in on the remaining space between myself and them. I have nowhere to go.

Reaching into my back pocket, I pull out my phone

and quickly FaceTime my brother. He answers immediately. I don't say a word and turn the camera around so that he can see what is happening. After a moment, I turn it back to me.

"They have me completely surrounded," I explain.

I see that he is already in his truck. "Get into your Jeep and lock the doors, I'm almost there."

Get into the Jeep, I ask myself why didn't I think of that? Turning, I get the door open just enough to get inside and then instantly lock it once it shuts.

Pulling the phone back up to my face, I say, "All right, I'm inside."

"Are you all right?"

"Yes, just wasn't expecting it. I didn't know they were there until they come up behind me."

I see it all over my brother's face. He wants to lecture me, but he isn't saying a word. I'm expecting the whole "I told you so" spiel but all I get is, "I'll be there in less than a minute."

Ending the call, all I can do is sit here and look around. Flash after flash bounces off the windows, I feel kind of silly just sitting here in my car.

Justin wasn't kidding. Not even a minute later, the group starts to part away and I see Justin pushing his way to my door.

Unlocking it, he opens it. "Move over," he demands. The pissed off look in his eyes doesn't go unnoticed.

Climbing over the center console, I sit down into the passenger seat as my brother takes the driver's seat.

I watch as he starts the Jeep and ever so slowly starts backing the vehicle out of the parking space. I'd never try this, but he is managing it like a pro and the reporters are slowly parting a path for us to move.

It takes some time, but as we pull out of the parking lot, I turn to see that they have followed us all the way to the street and are still taking pictures, of what I have no idea.

Looking over at Justin, he is looking straight forward and a very pissed off look is stretched across his face.

"Look…" I start but he cuts me off.

"No," he throws up his hand and signs.

He pulls into a parking lot of a shopping complex and throws the Jeep into park, now that pissed off set of eyes is looking right at me.

"What in the hell were you thinking?"

"I was thinking I was going to go and meet Megan for breakfast."

Justin stares at me for a moment. I can see the words flying through his head, he is just trying to pick the best ones to throw at me.

"Did you not see the picture this morning?"

Nodding, I confirm to him that I have seen it.

"Then why would you think it was a good idea to leave the house, Jordyn? That picture was taken right in front of your place, obviously someone knew where you lived or followed you and Asher yesterday. I wasn't going to get involved with this, but after today…you are moving into something with a gate in front of it."

I'm about to argue, but I realize I can't argue and say he can't tell me what to do, or that I'm a grown woman and can take care of myself, because obviously with what just happened, it's untrue. Instead I just nod my agreement, lean back in my seat and look out the front windshield.

I believe I've shocked my brother into stunned silence. Out of the corner of my eye, I see him just sitting there, staring at me.

"Where are we going now?" Looking back at Justin, I wait for him to respond.

"I thought about taking you to my place or Mom and Dad's, but I'm not sure if anyone is going to follow us, so next best place is Asher's, they can't get through the gates."

Justin doesn't wait for me to respond, he turns himself in the driver's seat, shifts into drive and in fifteen minutes we are pulling into Asher's driveway.

Asher is waiting in the threshold of his open front door when we pull up. Before I can open the door, he has walked down and opened it for me.

"Eventful morning?"

"You could say that. I'd love to say that I'm here to go to the lake with you today, but it looks like I'm going house hunting." I look over at Justin, who is still sitting in the driver's seat now sporting a smile that is grinding at my nerves.

Grabbing my hand, Asher kisses the top of it, and I bring my attention back to him.

"I'd be more than happy to go check out some places with you," his eyes go to Justin.

Bouncing a look between them, I realize this has been a conversation between them before now.

Changes, they have been pouring over my life this past week and it doesn't look to be stopping any time soon. I knew things were going to be intense when I joined the band. I knew some precautions were going to have to be made, one of the reasons I gave in to having my brother join the team as a bodyguard, but losing Mr. Emly, and now having to move, it's all getting to be a little over-whelming and I've no idea what I'm going to do if this bromance between my brother and my boyfriend continues to grow.

Looking straight out the windshield, I want nothing more than to be back in the warm bath from last night, hiding away in the words of my book.

Justin taps my arm and I turn, what I'm hoping is a very annoyed set of eyes, to look at him.

"Jordyn, everything is going to even out soon. Take a couple deep breaths, go check out some places. I have to get home, but let me know where you decide and we'll get all the moving details handled together."

My phone vibrates, it's a text from Megan.

Megan: Where are you?

Crap, I forgot to let her know what was going on.

I tap the box to respond, but Asher gets my attention first, "Were you supposed to meet her?"

"Yes, for breakfast about forty-five minutes ago."

"Tell her we are on our way, I was going to suggest we go grab something anyway. I'm sure she is going to want to go with us today anyway."

Me: Sorry, will explain when I get there, on my way.

Turning back to my brother, I say, "Thank you for the rescue, I'll talk to you later."

His hand goes up to stop me, "One last thing, the two of you might want to remember in public to cool the kisses down, it's getting harder for me to ignore them and not want to play the big brother role."

His stare goes straight past me to Asher, I can't help the smile that stretches across my face. "I was wondering how long it would take for you to say something about the picture."

"Me, wait until you see Dad again, if for anything you two better cool it for his sake."

CHAPTER THIRTY-TWO

ASHER

"I honestly didn't think anyone was around to worry about," I try to defend the reason behind the heated kiss yesterday as I dropped off Jordyn.

When I saw the post this morning, I was waiting for the call from Justin. I didn't expect him to be letting me know that he would be dropping Jordyn off. I was in the middle of getting dressed and heading to her place myself when I saw the new headline. It had meant that a reporter or someone had followed us and now knew where she lived. I was hoping to get there before they did, but that's not what happened at all. To no surprise, Justin was already a step ahead of me. He was already driving over there when she called him.

"Man, you know better than any of us, everything in public when you are in the spotlight is a perfect photo opportunity. They will be everywhere, it doesn't take them long to find what they are searching for."

Justin is right, "Sorry, I should have known to be more careful."

"Well, on the positive side," Jordyn cuts into our conversation, "I believe everyone is convinced that we are a real couple and it's not just a publicity stunt for the group."

"Yes, because that's what I was worried about," Justin rolls his eyes.

Taking Jordyn's hand into mine, she looks over to me, "Come on, we need to get going before Megan texts again."

We have looked at three different apartment complexes today since breakfast, and Jordyn has finally agreed on one not more than ten minutes from my house. It's larger than the place she has now, but I never thought about everything that would have to be done before she moved in until we're standing there and she's asking all the questions about the changes she is going to have to add to the place to accommodate for her not being able to hear, namely the smoke detectors and doorbell.

It has also been decided that she will stay with Megan until her place is ready, but I manage to convince her to stay with me for tonight.

Grilling up a couple of steaks, potatoes and vegetables for dinner, the night is too nice to spend inside. We enjoy dinner in my outside entertainment area next to the pool, with the fire light and just the two of us.

"You know right now, it's hard to believe the intensity

of our lives at this moment. It's so peaceful out here. The fire, the reflection from the water of the lights dancing around. I would say the quiet, but that's my world anyway," Jordyn laughs are her own comment.

"How are you holding up to all of this? I don't want you to give me an answer you think I want to hear, or to say you are fine. It's you and me, I want you to let me in a little. I still see the sadness in your eyes, which I'm not saying you shouldn't have, but I want you to know I'm here."

Jordyn's smile doesn't reach fully across her face, another sign that she is holding back.

"You know last night, I sat on my bed and cried for an hour. No one was around and everything hit me all at once. Then I was mad at myself for feeling ungrateful for everything I've had happen. This is all a rush, the interviews, the photo sessions, the cameras, being followed. All of the changes including now having to move, it's all a little overwhelming. Not going to lie, it has taken some effort not to lose it all again today and just sit down and cry. On the other side of it, though, I'm being given a chance that not many people are lucky enough to have. Mr. Emly passing has been one of the hardest things I've had to push through, but I know he would want me to enjoy everything that is happening at this time and for that reason I've told myself everything is going to be all right, and I'm going to take everything that is happening right now and live it fully, because if losing Mr. Emly has taught me nothing else, it's to appreciate everyone in your life."

"Jordyn, don't forget, breaking down isn't a sign of

weakness, it's all right to cry and mourn. If you need that time..."

Shaking her head, Jordyn stops me. "I've mourned and I'm not saying that it won't hit me one day and the tears can't be fought, but I'm not going to sulk and hide. This experience isn't easy, the road to fame, but I'm loving every step of it, and to have you next to me through the whole thing just makes it that much better."

Jordyn gets up from her chair and settles herself on my lap. Her fingers go into the hair at the back of my head and she takes my lips with hers. The kiss isn't demanding, but soft.

Pulling back, I look her straight in the eyes, "I want you to teach me to feel the music."

There it is, a true smile. No sadness behind it and her eyes shine. Standing, she reaches out for my hand. Taking hers, she leads me back into the house, and into my studio.

She turns to me, "Take off your shoes."

Without hesitation or questions, I do as she tells me to do.

"Most songs, be them soft or heavier, always have a beat. Be it the drums, the bass of the song, there is usually always a vibration you can feel." She points over to my ear plugs that I still have sitting on the counter from the other night, "Put those on again and close your eyes."

I do as I'm told and wait. Within a few moments I start to feel the vibration on the floor under my bare feet. I'm able to find the timing to the song that is playing pretty easily.

Opening my eyes, I find Jordyn standing right in front

of me, with a smile that has been missing for a few days now.

It takes a moment, but it's as though my entire body begins to pulse with the beat that is vibrating through the floor and into my bare feet.

Jordyn grabs my hand and puts it on her chest, her lips move, "Show me."

I tap with the beat of the song over her heart, keeping in time with the song. Her smile shines even brighter.

Jordyn takes a step closer to me, leaving no space in between us. She starts to sway with the beat I'm still tapping on her chest. With her other hand, she reaches up and takes one of the plugs out of my ears.

One of our slower songs, "It's for Me," is playing throughout the room and we are moving in perfect time with it.

"You found the beat," she kisses me lightly. "This is how I know a song has begun. There is more than just feeling the sounds to know the song. I download sheet music and the words and it's a lot of memorizing, but at least I can still image what the rhythm may be of a song."

"Do you remember the sounds the instruments make?"

She shrugs, "My answer would be yes, I believe I can imagine the sound still, but like anything you don't have for a length of time, you start to forget it. I'm sure what I still think the sound is in my head isn't quite right."

We continue to move together, I'm not ready to have her leave my arms, but her knowing little smile doesn't go unnoticed.

"What's with the smile?"

"The song is over."

She is right, it is, and I do realize now there isn't any vibration under my feet. "You don't always need music to dance."

"I thought maybe you were trying to test me."

"I'm the one being taught, why would I need to test you? I just like dancing with you, wasn't ready to let go. So, is our lesson over?"

She surprises me when her fingers go to the front of my shirt and start making work of the buttons, undoing each in its turn. Her eyes look up at me and they are starting to turn smoky.

Opening my shirt, she runs her hands over my chest, placing small kisses where her hands have already started a heated path on my skin. Her hands push my shirt off my shoulders and I drop my arms to allow it to drop to the floor.

Her lips start a path up my neck as her hands drop to my belt, making quick work of it and then releasing each button on my button-fly jeans. Her knuckles brush against the skin just above the band of my boxer briefs and I hear my own moan fill the studio.

"That sound is the one sound I wish I could hear and not only feel."

Her lips claim mine before I can respond. Her tongue finds mine. Backing her up a couple of steps until her back is against the wall, I raise her hands over her head, pinning them there with one hand.

Leaving her lips, I trail my lips down her neck, with my free hand I find the soft skin of her stomach under her shirt. Feeling her warm skin, up her waist and around to her back, I unclasp her bra. Pushing both garments up over her head, I release her hands for her to remove the clothing and allow them to join my shirt on the floor. Her hands come back to the waist of my pants as she starts to push them down over my hips, but with my body pinning hers to the wall, she can't manage to push them all the way off. Stepping back, I remove the rest of my clothing and then before she can move, I kneel down in front of her.

CHAPTER THIRTY-THREE

JORDYN

Asher drops to his knees in front of me and mine go weak. I lock my knees so that they don't go out from under me. His fingers go straight to work on the button and zipper of my pants, and when he starts to move them down my waist he freezes, his dark blue eyes staring at me in surprise.

"You aren't wearing any underwear."

Shaking my head, I give him what I hope is a teasing smile. "We were supposed to go to the lake today."

His eyes shine with a deeper need when he realizes my meaning behind my reasoning for not wearing any underwear today.

Asher quickly pushes my pants down over my legs, and helps me step out of them. His body rises against mine, pressing me hard against the wall as he makes his way back to his feet. His hand under my backside, he lifts me and my legs instantly wrap around his waist.

I think we are heading out to his room, but he surprises

me when he takes a couple steps back and sits us down on the bench, me now straddling him.

Lifting me slightly under the arms, he adjust himself until I feel his hardness slowly sliding into me. His lips find one breast and sucks it fully into his mouth. My head falls back, my hands pressing his head to me, begging for more.

His hands on my hips, he pushes me back, and then pulls me right back to him, each time I feel him a little deeper inside. I find the perfect rhythm on my own and his hands leave my waist to tangle in my hair.

When his mouth leaves my breast, I want to scream out in protest, but his lips find mine, his tongue demanding.

The need in my core slowly starts to build, my lips break away from his, my lungs in need of air. With my hands at the back of his neck, I demand his mouth to claim one of my breasts. The first touch of his tongue against my tight nipple and I'm about gone. I can feel myself tightening around him and my hips begin to move faster and faster.

He sucks hard and that's it. I'm sure his name is loud throughout the room as I find my release.

Asher's hands slide down to my hips once again, and he continues the pace I had started, the sensation of him being pulled in deeper and deeper with each wave of release is almost more than I can handle. An intense shockwave rocks my core and finally his arms tighten around me, holding me close to him as he finds his release.

We sit like this for a moment, our breathing in unison as we try to catch our breath.

After a little time, Asher looks up at me, "I'm not going to lie, I was planning on a little more teasing, but the whole no underwear thing did it."

Laughing, I kiss him.

"Jordyn, don't laugh," his hands are on my hips and pulling me tight into him.

Smiling down at him, I rock as much as his grasp will allow against him.

His eyes instantly change to the dark blue color and before I know what's happening, in one swift motion he stands, his hands supporting me under my backside. My legs wrap around his waist and I hold on as he walks us out of the studio and down to his room.

Together we fall onto the bed, this time him on top of me. I no longer have any control as his body presses me into the soft mattress.

He pulls his hips back just enough and then slowly pushes back into me. My hands fist into the comforter, as my body hasn't come completely down from my last release. I thrust my hips up to meet each of his movements.

I don't even realize I have shut my eyes until Asher taps on my temple. Opening them, I look straight up at him.

"Don't close your eyes, Jordyn. I want to watch you fall apart under me, I want you to keep your eyes on me the whole time."

"Asher," his name escapes again.

His name falling from my lips causes him to thrust harder and faster. I feel my release starting to build again.

His lips are moving but I have no idea what he is

saying. My brain is fogged over and his eyes have me hypnotized. It doesn't take long before we find our release for the second time tonight, together.

Saturday, we spend the whole day over at Jesse's house for his little girl, Jayline's, first birthday party. I finally have the chance to meet Jesse's wife, Kaitlyn, and Emily, Dawson's girlfriend. It's nice to have other women around, especially since Megan has come to the party as well, but it doesn't go unnoticed how much of the time she spends with Noah. Something I plan on chatting with her about once we are alone again.

Sitting around, laughing, eating, and enjoying time together, these new additions to my life are definitely starting to feel more like family. With days like this it's easy to forget the craziness that follows us around in the world outside of these gatherings.

The weekend has flown by, Megan has convinced me that we need a little girls' only time and I have to agree it is a good idea, with the exception that my brother is never too far away.

We go out to lunch, do a little shopping and are now getting our nails and toes done.

"So, are you excited about your new apartment?" Megan signs as we get our toes worked on.

Shrugging, I look back down and watch as the lady in front of me works the nail polish onto my toenails.

Megan reaches over and slaps my arm. "Come on, you have to be a little excited, your new place is amazing."

"I'm excited, but I liked the place I was living in."

"Change isn't a bad thing, Jordyn."

"I know that, but when there is so much of it at one time, it gets a little overwhelming."

"You are handling it well."

Smiling over at my friend, I'm not so sure if I agree with her.

"How are things going with you and Asher? I was supposed to have a roommate these past few days, but if I'm counting correctly, last night was the first night at my house."

"I know, I'm sorry, I'll be there tonight as well."

Megan laughs, rolling her eyes, "I don't blame you, I would be staying with my hot boyfriend as well. I'm a little surprised it wasn't offered for you just to move in with him as much as you two are together."

My heart completely belongs to Asher, I've no doubt in my feeling for him, but I think moving in would have been a little fast.

"I still want my own space. I don't think we are at that stage yet. Everything else is moving pretty fast, this I would rather take a little slower."

"Slower, right," Megan's expression is full of sarcasm as she signs.

"I know, I know. I just think for now this is better."

"Well, speaking of changes happening fast, you get to be in your apartment tomorrow for one night and we leave on Wednesday for the festival. Are you excited?"

"More like terrified. This will be my first time on stage

with the group, and it's not a small group of people we are playing for."

"You are going to do great. I have finished training my replacement for my previous job, I'm officially all yours."

Looking away from my best friend, I concentrate on the little design the lady in front of me is putting on my big toe. There is so much that can be lost if this doesn't go well, Megan quit her job for me, new place that if I hadn't just signed a contract with the band, I'd never be able to afford.

Megan grabs the short sleeve of my shirt and pulls, getting my attention, "Stop. I see it all over your face."

Looking past her, I see my brother sitting on a bench just out front of the salon. He too has given things up for this.

Waving her hand in front of my face to get me to focus on her, Megan signs, "Look, get it all out now. That's what I'm here for. Being the best friend, I'm allowed to see your insecurities and know when you are scared, but let me tell you this. You deserve this and you will be amazing. Stop worrying about all of us around you, even if for some strange and far off reason this doesn't work out, none of us will be disappointed. For the record, though, I fully believe you are going to rock this popularity thing, you were meant to perform, Jordyn, and you are showing so many people out there that nothing should hold you back from your dreams. You are a deaf person living out your dream of singing, you are going to be an inspiration to so many people."

I fight the tears forming behind my eyes and smile at

Megan. I'm so thankful for this woman in my life. "You have to say all of that, you are my best friend."

"No, the perfect part of being a best friend is I get to be honest with you. Get it all out now, because as soon we walk out of this place I'm expecting my strong-minded, stubborn, go-getting best friend back. We are going to get ready to fly out Wednesday and you are going to start the new chapter of your life and be amazing at it. I mean every woman wants to be you right now, look who your boyfriend is," she turns her phone toward me and shows me one of the many images flying around social media nowadays of Asher and myself.

Smiling, I wipe the single tear that has managed to escape. "He is hot."

"And you are gorgeous. You guys make a hot couple."

At the top of her screen a white box flashes with a notification that she has received a text from Noah. Now is the perfect time.

"Speaking of couples, what is going on between you and Noah?" I ask.

Megan pulls her phone back and swipes the screen, then quickly closes it and places it back on her lap, this time screen down.

"What, aren't you going to answer Noah's text?" I tease her.

It's not often I see Megan blush and right now her cheeks are definitely a shade of red.

"So you can ask all the questions you want about Asher and me, but you're not going to respond when I ask you about Noah," I continue my teasing.

Megan has never shied away from telling me about a

guy she is dating. Something is definitely going on if she is staying quiet about this one.

I watch as she takes in a deep breath and finally her eyes have that "give-in" look to them. Her hands finally come up, "There is nothing going on, we just text back and forth."

"Nothing going on? At the photoshoot you guys were all chatty, and then Saturday over at Jesse's I don't think there was a moment you two were apart, and you want me to believe you two are only texting?"

Megan shrugs and there is something in her expression that I don't think I've ever see in my friend's face when it comes to a guy, it's almost like she is disappointed, rejected. I'm not sure of the word I'm looking for.

"I'm not lying to you, we are only really texting."

"You know the guys say he is the playboy of the group, right?" I feel that I have to warn her, although I'm sure it's no big secret or anything.

"That's the thing, he doesn't act like that when we are talking. The problem is we are only talking, he hasn't asked me out or anything."

"Since when do you wait for a guy to ask you out? You aren't usually shy."

Again, Megan shrugs, "I don't know, it's different with Noah."

I'm getting to know the guys, but I don't know them enough to give out any advice on any of them. Noah does have a sweet side of him. Most of the time he is goofing off, or teasing, but there have been times I've seen a very soft side of him. I can see what Megan sees in him.

"I wish I had advice to give you, do you want me to talk to him?"

She shakes her head, "No, please don't say anything. He might just be looking at me in the friend zone and I'm just thinking he wants a little more. Please keep this between the two of us."

"I won't say anything, but just to let you know, I'm not the only one who has noticed the two of you in the group. Comments have been made."

Megan rolls her eyes and sits herself back against the chair, she doesn't say anything else, but brings her phone up to look at. I'm taking that as a sign that this conversation is done.

It's eight in the morning and I'm standing in the middle of my new apartment, bags packed. Looking around, I have to admit this place is amazing. The large great room makes the place feel huge. All top brand appliances, the colors are grey and white, giving it a very clean feel and look. My mom insisted on new furniture, so I gave in and let her go crazy. I don't have one ounce of ability to decorate, my mother, on the other hand, missed her calling and should have been a decorator. It has two bedrooms, and two and a half baths, one in each room and a half in the hallway. Right off the great room is a separate formal dining room, which I converted into my music room with my piano and guitars.

The place is probably way too big for just one person, but if I'm being honest, I love it. Motion to my right catches my attention, turning I see Megan coming out of the spare room.

"This place is great. That shower is amazing, I may have to move in with you."

Last night Megan insisted on staying my first night with me, I think Asher had the same plan and was disappointed when Megan made the announcement that she was staying after we moved a few last-minute things into the apartment.

"Just got the text," she continued as she wheeled her bags out, "the car is downstairs and the driver is headed up to help with the bags."

Grabbing my backpack off the couch, I grab the handle of one suitcase and open the door just as the driver and one of the group's bodyguards approaches the door.

"Good morning, Jacob," I greet the band's guard.

He smiles a greeting at me and reaches for my suitcases.

Megan and I follow the two men down to the car. The rest of the guys have already been picked up and are waiting inside when we get in.

Zayden moves over and gives me room next to Asher.

He kisses me lightly when I sit down, "Are you ready?"

Taking a deep breath, I smile, "As ready as I can be."

Once everyone is settled, we are on our way to the airport.

I see everyone chatting away, Noah and Megan are in some sort of conversation, but with so much going on I don't pay too much attention.

Asher taps on my leg, when I look over he is pointing at Jesse.

"I was wondering how you liked your first night in your new place?" Jesse asks.

"It's larger than my last one, but so far I like it."

"We are having a party when we get back, right?" Jesse smiles.

"Absolutely, I'd love to have everyone come over. Plenty of room."

The interviews, the photoshoots, and the recording times, all of these things made this all seem very real, but nothing beats the feeling of getting out of this car with the whole band, our bodyguards all around us and all of the people out front of the airport. This crowd put the crowds in front of the studios to shame. The airport security is doing well with keeping everyone back, as we are guided through them to the entrance of the airport.

CHAPTER THIRTY-FOUR

ASHER

I watch Jordyn as we are moved through the crowd, her head is down, but I see her eyes looking around from the sides. I have her hand, she seems relaxed. This experience is what fame is all about. We have had a couple crowds in the past couple of weeks, but nothing is going to compare to what's going to happen in the next couple of days. The rush of excitement is hard to explain, you have to live it to understand it.

The flight itself is the quietest part of our day. Leaving the airport is about the same as when we arrived back at the last one, but the crowd out in front of the hotel is something you have to witness. There are fans along with reporters. Pictures are being shoved at us to sign, hands are grabbing from everywhere. Justin met us at the airport and is with us now, but with him already committing to a job with the festival itself, he won't be with us once the events begin.

We aren't taken straight up to the rooms, but to a

conference room that Scott has set up to go over the schedule for the next couple of days.

Once inside, everyone finds a seat.

"Man, I've missed this, what a rush." Noah plops down into a chair, grabbing a bottle of water from the table.

"Welcome," the manager of the hotel greets us, "we have set out a selection of food for you and hope that you will enjoy your stay with us."

Scott finishes the conversation with the manager as we begin to fill plates with the food that has been provided.

I watch Jordyn and Megan as they sign back and forth between the two of them. I've realized when there is a lot of activity going on in a room, they resort to signing only.

Jordyn seems relaxed, maybe a little excited. Her smile is stretched across her face and her eyes have a little twinkle to them.

"All right, guys," Scott comes back into the room from speaking to the manager. "We have tonight free only and then it's go mode from there. Tomorrow, we have another television interview and a couple radio spots, then Friday we are at the festival with fan meet and greets and interviews as well. Saturday morning we have soundcheck and then you guys are on Saturday evening."

"So what you are saying is enjoy the rest of the day," Noah speaks up.

"As long as it's here at the hotel, sure. You have the pool, enjoy a day of relaxing. For dinner tonight, the hotel it providing a private room down at their restaurant." Scott makes sure all of us understand we are to stay here.

I look over at Justin, we have already made plans for

something today and I want to make sure everything is still happening. He knows what my questioning look is about and he nods, confirming everything is a go.

"Sweet, an afternoon at the pool sounds perfect," Megan nods at Jordyn for confirmation.

"You guys finish up here, schedules and times have all been sent over to you, dinner tonight is at seven." Scott is up and out of the room before anyone else can say a word.

Turning to Jordyn, I grab her hand, she looks over at me from her conversation with Megan.

"Hey, before we settle down at the pool, I have somewhere I would like to take you."

She gives me a confused look, "Didn't Scott just inform us we were to stay here?"

I wave my hand in the air to dismiss her concern, "Don't worry, it's already been cleared by the boss."

"All right, when do we leave?"

"Right after you finish eating."

Jordyn looks over at Megan, "I'll meet you down at the pool when I get back." She turns her head back to me, "I'm ready now."

Taking her hand, I get Justin's attention and the three of us leave the room.

Justin leads us down to the parking structure that is under the hotel.

"Why didn't we get dropped off down here?" Jordyn asks as Justin leads us to the car waiting.

"Even though all of that is crazy, it's kind of necessary. You have to show up to the public, allow the pictures to be taken, sign a couple of pictures that are shoved at you. We don't want to hide every time we go somewhere, that starts all types of rumors."

"We aren't hiding and they are creating rumors," Jordyn rolls her eyes.

"There will always be rumors," Justin points out as he opens the back door to the borrowed SUV for Jordyn and I to climb in, then he takes his place behind the wheel.

Once daylight shines through the windows, Jordyn is looking all around, trying to get any clue she can as to where we are going.

I'm hoping that smile stays with her through all of this.

When we pull up to the gates to the backstage of the festival, Jordyn looks over at me confused. "What are we doing here?"

I catch Justin's eyes in the rearview mirror, I hope this works out the way we were looking at it to.

"I wanted to show you the stage. Show you what you will be looking out onto. The next couple of days are going to be pretty busy and today only the setup crews are around, so I thought this would be the best day to stop by and show you."

Justin pulls the SUV over by the entrance gates after being directed where to park and we all three get out. Taking Jordyn's hand, I lead her up to the largest stage at the festival. Justin is following behind, but on his phone, sending the text.

I direct Jordyn up the stairs and follow her onto the stage we'll be performing on. I follow her but stop at the top of the stairs and watch as she walks to the middle of the stage.

Justin comes to stand next to me, "Everything is ready, the guys should be pulling up in a couple of minutes, they weren't that far behind us."

"This is a good idea, right?" I ask Justin, starting to second-guess our decision to do this.

"Scott said this was requested, we have to just be here for her."

I watch the smile on Jordyn's face as she looks around the stage and then out to the open field in front of the stage. She walks over to the edge and just stands there.

Walking over, I stand next to her, and she looks over at me. "It's hard to believe the amount of people that will be out there," I look over the empty area that will soon be shoulder-to-shoulder people in a couple of days.

"You know, I thought I would be more nervous, but it feels right. Don't get me wrong, I'm sure there will be jitters the night we go on, but I need to be here, I need to do this."

Justin walks over. "It's time."

Jordyn looks around. "Time for what?"

My heart is pounding in my chest, that smile she has, I want to keep it there but I have no idea how she is going to take all of this. Taking her hand, I walk her over to a stool that has been placed in the middle of the stage. I have her sit facing the large screen that serves as a backdrop to the bands performing.

I give her a small kiss. "There is another reason we have brought you out here. Please know I'm right here," I let go of her hand and take a step back behind her, then nod to Justin.

The large screen flashes and a video with Sean shines on it. I hear Jordyn's intake of breath and then the sob, and I have to fight to not close the space between us and take her in my arms.

Sean's voice fills the empty space around us. "Jordyn, look at this, we are on the big stage together. I remember the first day you walked into my music room, this little girl with a very large dream. Your eyes were so sad because you were without the ability to hear. Through those sad little eyes I saw complete determination, that's how I knew you would be here. I'm sorry I'm not standing next to you for this new adventure, but know I'm always going to be by your side. With each beat of the drum, the strum of the guitar, the wave of sounds that hums through you from the piano, they are all the extension of what I've taught you so that you can grab that dream."

I have to ball my fists to keep them from reaching out to the woman who has completely changed my world as her body shakes from the tears that are pouring down her face. I have to fight my own tears as I never had the chance to tell Sean thank you for bringing this woman to our group.

Justin is fighting it with every muscle in his body as well with each sob that escapes his sister's body. She needs to hear this, but it's hard to stand back and watch.

The rest of the group is now standing with me, my brother places his hand on my shoulder for the extra strength I need to stay back while Sean's voice continues.

"I would say please, no tears, but I have no idea why

people say that. It's all right to cry, but let it be for now and then dry them up and enjoy what I know will be the time of your life. Jordyn, this is your chance to show people how to feel the music, you are the perfect person to show the world that nothing should hold you back from what your heart wants to do. Now, stand up."

Jordyn does as he tells her to do.

"Now turn around, your family is waiting for you."

She turns and stumbles back a little when she finds myself, the band, Megan, Scott and Justin all standing together.

"Jordyn..."

Megan signs for her to turn back around to the screen.

Sean signs, and Megan translates out loud for the rest of us, "I'm so very proud of you and love you very much, now go show the world how to feel the music."

The screen goes dark and we stand by and wait. Jordyn has a hand on the stool she was sitting on and she hasn't looked away from the screen.

After a few more moments I look over at Justin and tip my head in Jordyn's direction. As much as I want to be the one to hold her, I think she needs her brother right now.

We watch as Justin walks to stand in front of her. His hands move as he signs something to her, but it's between the two of them. Jordyn slightly nods her head at whatever her brother is saying to her and then crashes into his chest.

It takes a couple of minutes but Jordyn, still tucked close to her brother's side, turns to us. "I can't put into words how much this means to me. Scott, you gave me a chance that not many others would have done, and you guys have opened your arms to a new member of the group."

"Jordyn," Dean is the one to say something first, "when something fits right then the change is good. You belong with this group, we were good before, but we are now reaching for great."

"Thank you, Dean, I hope to not let you guys down. I do want to thank you guys for putting this together. It was hard, but I needed it. I know Sean is with me, but it's kind of the goodbye we really didn't get to have."

Jordyn takes a couple of deep breaths and then pulls away from her brother's embrace. She walks over and together we all surround her in a group hug, well, except Scott, he smiles from the side, though.

I'm sure that video was hard for him, he and Sean have been friends for years. Sean had sent him that video right before he passed away, asking him to show it to Jordyn when she arrived here. He set the whole thing up as a last request from a friend.

Jordyn surprises me when the circle pulls apart and she is left in the center. "I think it's time we head back and go spend a little time by the pool."

Proof that she is all right, she is ready to keep that beaming smile and move on with this weekend's activities. I even see the relief in Justin's eyes, we weren't sure how she was going to come away from this video, but we knew she needed to see it.

CHAPTER THIRTY-FIVE

JORDYN

The rest of this week has been flying by. I feel a certain calm after seeing the video message from Mr. Emly. It was heart breaking to see him, alive and talking to me, knowing that I would never have that again, but I'm glad he left it for me.

Yesterday was a day filled with interviews. It was a day of go here, finish, move to the next, and then repeat. All of the interviews are basically the same and are feeling pretty natural now. Today, however, I'm very excited for.

We are going over to the festival to meet with fans and sign autographs. This is something I haven't had a lot of experience in yet. Back home, every once in a while we would get someone coming up to the table at a restaurant and asking for one, but nothing like they have described today will be like.

We all meet down in the lobby and then together we are shuffled through the door out to the front of the hotel where we are greeted by reporters and fans. I'm starting to understand everything a little more.

Once at the festival, we are directed back to a behind the scenes location, where I have to admit, I have a few fan girl moments myself with some of the bands and country artists that are back here.

We are set up in a couple different location for an hour each time, three times throughout the day. Food is laid out for everyone.

We are on our second round of meet and greets when a girl comes up to the table in front of me, probably close to ten or eleven years old.

She hands me a picture of the group and then signs, "Can you please sign this for me?"

Tears instantly filled my eyes, she is deaf.

Her mom, who is standing behind her, leans forward, "She has been so excited to meet you."

"Your name is what?" I sign.

She spells out, "E-M-M-A."

"It's nice to meet you."

"You are deaf like me." Her little smile is huge across her face.

"Yes, I am." I sign my name to the group photo she has handed me.

Getting up from the table, I start to make my way around it. One of our bodyguards follows me, but no one tries to stop me.

Making my way over to the girl and her mother, I give the girl a hug and we pose for a picture together. I want nothing more than to take more time and talk to the girl, but I know there are a lot of people waiting for their turn.

"How would you like a picture with all of us?" I ask her.

Her eyes light up as her head bobs up and down. I wave for the rest of the group to join me. It takes a little extra time but that's what we are here to do.

Once everyone finds their seats again, I signal for Scott to come over.

"Do we have any front row passes laying around by chance?"

Scott smiles and pulls two laminated passes out of his inside jacket pocket hanging off of a Driven Roads lanyard. "How about front row and backstage?"

I watch as her mother translates Scott's words and the girls face lights up. "Thank you," she signs and then throws her arms around my waist and hugs me.

They moved along and I turned to Scott, "Thank you."

"You know, that gave me an idea that I should have thought about a while ago, we may need to start having a signing interpreter join us for concerts on stage."

"It's funny you say that because you already have one working for you. Megan is amazing at signing songs, and she knows all of ours."

"I believe I need to go and speak to Megan," Scott turns and goes back behind the stage, I'm sure in search for Megan.

Rounding the large table again, I sit back down in my seat next to Asher, he finishes signing the picture in front of him and hands it back to the teenage girl standing there then turns his attention to me.

"So how did that feel?"

My face is starting to hurt from the huge smile I have, "There are no words to describe that feeling."

It's finally here, tonight is the night. This is a moment I've been dreaming about since I was very little. My hair and makeup have been done and right now I'm just sitting here alone in my dressing room. Holy crap, I'm in my dressing room! My nerves are blooming a little more with each minute that ticks by. I've ran through the songs a million times I think, but I'm still worried I'm going to forget words, or miss a sign from Asher on when to start that we have worked hours on.

The door to my room opens and through the mirror in front of me I see Megan. She too has had hair and makeup done and her outfit looks amazing on her. Now that she is going to be on stage with us, she needs to look the part as well.

"Why aren't you dressed yet?" she signs and then shuts the door behind her.

"You look amazing."

"Thank you. I'm not going to lie, I'm a little nervous and wish I had a little more time to make sure I have all of the songs down before I have to go on stage and sign all of them."

"You are kidding, right? Megan, you had every song this band sings memorized way before I signed any contracts. You'll be great."

"I've peeked at the crowds out there. There are no words to describe the sounds that are filling the whole park. It's amazing. You are going to love the energy."

"Besides the sound of Asher's voice, I don't think there is any other sound I'd want to hear more than the roar of a crowd out in front of the stage."

"Trust me, you are going to feel it and it's going to be just as powerful." She turns and grabs my clothes off the rack and hands them to me, "You better get dressed, Ms. Collins, your fans await."

Backstage and we are waiting for them to announce us. I can feel the energy all around us, at times I swear I can feel a vibration under my feet.

Asher takes my hand, and I look up at him.

"How are you doing?"

This is the first chance since soundcheck this afternoon that we have really seen each other. He is bouncing slightly on his toes and I'm wondering if he still gets nervous before a concert.

"Are you nervous?" I ask without answering his question.

"Nope, just excited to get on stage again."

I watch him for a moment trying to gauge his action, and still feel there is something else there, but I push it out of my mind.

A pair of hands on my shoulders have me looking behind me, it's Justin.

"How are you holding up back here?" he signs.

"A little nervous, but more excited. Just hoping I don't mess anything up."

"Well, I just came back to tell you, Mom and Dad along with Amber are here and sitting in their spots that

Scott arranged for them. They said to tell you good luck and that they will see you after the concert. Dad is beaming out there, just to let you know. I think he has walked the whole crowd informing all of them that you are his daughter."

Asher pulls slightly on my arm, bringing my attention to him before I can say anything to my brother. "It's time, let's go."

I turn for one last look at my brother as I follow Asher over to the stairs leading up to the stage. Justin smiles and points a finger up, reminding me that I'm not going to be alone. My eyes sting with tears for a moment but I take a couple deep breaths and smile back.

The stage is dark when we walk up and the lights have been turned off over the crowd. All I can see is the silhouette of heads out in front of us. Asher lets go of my hand, but doesn't go far, and Megan takes her place right off to my right. She'll be signing the introduction to me so that I know what's going on and then take her place on the right far side of the stage to perform the songs to the crowd.

There is a hum vibrating through my chest and I'm going to assume it's from the cheers of the crowd. Closing my eyes, I try to imagine in my head what it may sound like. A tap on my arm brings me to open my eyes again.

"Are you ready? They are starting the announcement," Megan lets me know.

All I can do is nod. I'm sure if I raised my hand right now she would see how nervous I am.

I watch her hands as she begins the introduction:

"Ladies and gentlemen, let's hear it for your favorite country band on the charts today, Driven Roads."

Lights start to flash around the stage, while the crowd lights stay off. The stage under my feet bounces, signaling to me that Dean has started on the drums. The vibration in my chest seems to intensify as the music starts, I look over at Megan.

She signs to me that the crowd is going insane.

Someone grabs my hand and I jump. Looking over, Asher is standing there looking straight at me. He nods and his hand leaves mine and takes place on his chest. He smiles at me and that's when a calm comes over me. This is it and he is right here beside me. I watch the tap of his hand against his chest as though it's in slow motion. I count it off, bringing my hand up to my chest to mirror his beat.

He smiles as he brings the mic up to his mouth. The first word he sings, the lights everywhere come on, but I can't look away from him just yet. I sing along with him in my head, finding the words and timing to the song. Taking a deep breath, I bring my mic up and realize, it's my time, it's the moment I've dreamed of and this is so much more than I could have ever imagined, but it's completely where I'm supposed to be.

My words begin as my part comes into the song and I'm finally able to turn and look out onto the sea of fans in front of us. What a rush. With the lights that are shining down onto the stage from in front of us, it only allows us to really see maybe the first ten or so rows well, after that it's just an outline of movement throughout the fans.

I spot my parents and can't look at them long for I may choke up looking at the pride they both have as they look up at me.

The moment that does it for me, though, and I find myself tearing up a little is when I see Emma up front with her mom, standing right in front of where Megan is standing, signing along with her.

Walking to the front of the stage, never missing a beat or word to the song we are singing I tap the shoulder of my brother, who demanded he be one of the guards standing in front of the stage as we performed, and motion for him to get Emma and bring her on stage.

Justin pulls the barrier apart, allowing the girl to walk through and then directs her onto the stage with us. I meet her at the top of the stairs, grabbing her hand and walking back toward Asher.

Placing my mic on the stage, I stand face to face with her and instead of singing the song with Asher, I begin to sign it with Emma. Together we show the crowd what the deaf world and music looks like.

We are just rounding off our last song and I know time wise it's been about an hour and a half, but it feels like only minutes. I'm not ready to leave the stage.

Asher takes my hand and together we move to the center of the stage. This is where I'm expecting the final words that Asher was supposed to say, but I'm surprised when Megan walks over to stand next to Asher and faces me as though she is going to translate.

Asher kisses my hand and turns to the crowd, I look over at Megan with a confused questioning look on my face.

She just smiles and her hands come up as I'm guessing Asher begins to talk.

She signs, "We have one more song we would like to perform before we go tonight, it's something new the band has been practicing."

My smile drops and I start to panic a little, what new song? I haven't learned a new song.

Asher looks away from the crowd and back at me, he hands Megan his microphone and I almost drop my mic when his hands come up and he signs my name sign.

Asher is signing and Megan is speaking his words out to the crowd.

"Jordyn, it's no secret how much you mean to me. You have taught me so much more about music and showed me a world beyond the sounds around us. The people have seen countless pictures of how much you mean to me, but I hope this song that I have written you will show you how much I love you. You have my heart."

My hands are shaking and my knees feel like they are going to give out from under me, there are tears streaming down my face and all I can do is stand here amazed and falling deeper in love with the man in front of me, who just communicated with me through my language.

Asher grabs the mic once again from Megan and signals to Zayden, who on guitar starts the song.

Asher doesn't look out into the crowd, he holds my hand tight in his and his eyes stay locked with mine as I watch his lips sing his song.

I can see you
From across the room
That look in your eyes

The move of your hands
As they follow through
Saying so much more
Than my words convey
You're getting under my skin
You're In every breath I take.
You're in every breath I take
With every move you make
feeling so much more
than words
Can ever say
It's just your way
But girl you've pulled me in
So deep and so far,
getting under my skin,
In every breath I take...
You're gentle touch
Showing how you form
The words I sing
Breathing life into me
Like I've never known
You may not hear my words
But feel my heart
It beats only for you
Even when we're apart
You're in every breath I take
With every move you make
feeling so much more
than words
Can ever say
It's just your way

But girl you've pulled me in
So deep and so far,
getting under my skin,
In every breath I take...
You're in every breath I take
With every move you make
feeling so much more
than words
Can ever say
It's just your way
But girl you've pulled me in
So deep and so far,
getting under my skin,
In every breath I take...

(You can hear Asher's song - Every Breath I Take on YouTube on Author Tonya Clark Channel)

The song ends and Asher pulls me close to him, placing my hand onto his chest right above his heart. "That beat belongs to you, Jordyn, it's our song."

I don't care if the whole world is watching or what pictures and words fly through social media tomorrow, I kiss Asher like we are the only two people in the world right now.

Asher ends the kiss and takes a step back, releasing my hand. His hand comes up with the sign for I love you, as he says the words into his mic.

I bring the mic up, "I love you, too."

Asher takes my hand once again and kisses it, before

he turns the two of us to the crowd, at this time the rest of the guys have joined us at the front of the stage.

The fans are going insane, the constant hum is a welcoming and exciting feeling. Asher releases my hand and I watch as he signs and his lips move as he looks out into the large crowd of fans, "We are Driven Roads. Goodnight, everyone."

And the lights go out.

ACKNOWLEDGMENTS

There are no words I can use to say thank you enough to Tana Perry and her husband Andy Ray Perry for writing and bringing to life the song in this book, Every Breath I Take. You two are an amazing couple and this book wouldn't have been complete without this song.

ABOUT THE AUTHOR

Tonya Clark lives in Southern California with her hot firefighter hubby and two amazing daughters. She writes contemporary romance featuring second chance, sports, MC, shifters, suspense, and deaf culture-inspired by her youngest daughter.

When not hiding in the office writing, Tonya has the amazing job of photographing hot cover models, coaching multiple soccer teams, and running her day job.

Tonya believes everyone deserves their Happily Ever After!

Sign-up for Tonya's newsletter at www.tonyaclarkbooks.com for book news and you can find all of her books on Amazon.

Join Tonya's Teasers reader group - facebook.com/groups/tonyasteasers facebook.com/authortonyaclark

instagram.com/authortonyaclark

bookbub.com/authors/tonya-clark

goodreads.com/authortonyaclark

amazon.com/author/tonyaclark

ALSO BY TONYA CLARK

<u>Sign of Love Series</u>

Silent Burn

Silent Distraction

Silent Protection

Silent Forgiveness

<u>Sign of Love Circle</u>

Shift

For the Love of Brayden

<u>Colorado Storm Series</u>

Slide Tackled

Game Plan

<u>Station 26 Series</u>

Shame on You

Shame on July

<u>Lunch Time Reads</u>

Healing Tristan

Mistletoe Hero

<u>Standalone</u>

Retake

Entangled Rivals

Hidden Flight

Scan For More Books By